HEAVEN'S A LIE

ALSO BY WALLACE STROBY

Some Die Nameless
The Devil's Share
Shoot the Woman First
Kings of Midnight
Cold Shot to the Heart
Gone 'Til November
The Heartbreak Lounge
The Barbed-Wire Kiss

HEAVEN'S A LIE

A novel

WALLACE STROBY

MULHOLLAND BOOKS

Little, Brown and Company
New York   Boston   London

Mulholland Books / Little, Brown and Company
Hachette Book Group
1290 Avenue of the Americas, New York, NY 10104
mulhollandbooks.com

First Edition: April 2021

Mulholland Books is an imprint of Little, Brown and Company, a division of Hachette Book Group, Inc. The Mulholland Books name and logo are trademarks of Hachette Book Group, Inc.

The publisher is not responsible for websites (or their content) that are not owned by the publisher.

The Hachette Speakers Bureau provides a wide range of authors for speaking events. To find out more, go to hachettespeakersbureau.com or call (866) 376-6591.

ISBN 978-0-316-54060-5
Library of Congress Control Number: 2020952886

Printing 1, 2021

LSC-C

Printed in the United States of America

Freedom is nothing but the distance
between the hunter and the hunted.

—Bei Dao

HEAVEN'S A LIE

ONE

———

WATCHING THROUGH THE office window, Joette knows the BMW won't make the curve.

Just past the motel, the highway hooks left across Taylor Creek. The car's going too fast. A squeal of brakes, a brief screaming skid, and it hits the bridge's right-side abutment head-on. Momentum spins the car around, pieces of it flying away across the blacktop. It comes to rest sideways in the road, pointing at the motel, steam hissing from under the buckled hood. The office window rattles a final time.

Later, it will occur to her that if she'd called 911 then—her cell phone right there on the desk—everything that happened after would have been different.

Instead, she's out the door without thinking. The hood is pushed back almost to the windshield, the glass cracked and sagging. The driver is slumped over the deflated airbag. The rear window's been blown out, and the trunk's open. Cubes of safety glass litter the ground.

She pulls at the driver's door latch. The door's wedged tight, bent in its frame. The driver raises his head, looks at her blankly through the window, eyes unfocused. He's wearing an army field jacket, has a shaved head and a full beard, gothic lettering across his throat.

She hears the fire before she sees it. An ominous pop and hiss, then a crackle of flame in the engine compartment. Fuel line rupture, she thinks, gasoline hitting hot metal.

Black smoke starts to pour from the engine. More flame. It won't take long for the fire to spread back through the car, reach the gas tank.

The driver is fumbling weakly with his shoulder harness. She pulls harder on the latch, and the door opens suddenly, sends her falling back onto the blacktop. Flames leap from the engine.

Get away, she thinks. *This whole thing's going up any second.*

The car begins to fill with noxious smoke. He makes an animal sound, and she sees the first flames come through the dashboard vents.

You can't leave him there.

She scrambles to her feet, leans into the open door. He grabs at her and she elbows his hands away, untwists the shoulder harness and pushes the red release button. The belt pops loose, retracts fast, and his weight falls against her. She hooks her arms under his, tries to pull him out, but can't get leverage.

You're both gonna burn.

Flames curl from under the dashboard, snap at the sleeve of her flannel shirt. The material begins to blacken and char. She slaps at it, feels the sting. Holding her breath against the smoke, she bear-hugs him from behind, throws her weight backward. He groans, seems to resist, then falls sideways out of the seat and onto the ground. She drags him away.

Sudden pain in her lower back. She ignores it, grips the collar of his jacket with both hands. Smoke hides most of the car now, lashing flame at the center of it. The seats are on fire. She pulls him into the lot, almost up to the office door, before finally letting go.

Something sails across her line of vision, glowing faintly. It flutters down and lands at her feet. When she picks it up, she sees it's a hundred-dollar bill, half of Benjamin Franklin's face burned away.

The driver coughs, and the blood on his lips is almost black. He lifts a weak hand, points to the car, mumbles something she can't understand.

Is there someone else in there?

She doesn't want to go back, get any closer to the fire, the heat.

You have to see.

She drops the bill, approaches the car, arm raised in front of her face, the heat keeping her back. Smoke pours through the rear window, but she can tell the backseat is empty.

She sees it then, inside the open trunk. A gray canvas gear bag lying on its side, packs of cash and a few loose bills spilling out.

The heat is a wall in front of her, shimmering the air. She knows the gas tank is just below the trunk. The fire will set it off any minute.

She leans into the heat, sweeps the packs and bills into the bag, grips its handles and backs away fast.

The tank goes up just as she reaches the lot. No explosion, just a loud *whump*, and heat coming at her like a wave. Fire sweeps through the car in a final rush, heat distorting the air, black smoke billowing higher into the blue winter sky. The tires pop like gunshots, one after the other. She stumbles back, trips and sits down hard.

The driver coughs again, more blood. His left hand is under the jacket, pressed against his stomach through his T-shirt. Blood pulses through his fingers. His jeans are dark with it, down to his knees.

He didn't get that in the accident. That's something else.

He looks at her, shudders twice and goes still. His eyes are open.

A wind springs up from nowhere, feeds the fire. The air smells of burning plastic and rubber. She sits there alongside the dead man and the bag full of money, watching the car burn, ash drifting down around them like black snow.

TWO

THE FIRE HAD all but burned itself out before the emergency vehicles arrived. Now she stands at the desk behind the counter, watching them winch the blackened skeleton of the car onto a flatbed. The bare rims scrape the roadway, the winch clanking and whining.

Two state police cars are in the lot, along with three local cruisers from Wall Township, all parked at angles, blocking in her Subaru. The local cops talk among themselves, nothing to do now. She can hear radio chatter from their cruisers.

Chaney, the state trooper, is sitting in one of the plastic chairs by the glass door, writing in a notebook. He looks tired and bored.

"How many?" he says.

"How many what?"

"Units."

"Ten."

Her left forearm throbs. One of the paramedics had cut away part of the sleeve, put salve on the burn and wrapped it with gauze and tape. She'd turned down his offer to call another ambulance, take her to the hospital, not wanting them to know she had no insurance. He'd seen the old crosswise scars on her wrist, pale against the skin, but hadn't mentioned them.

"How many occupied?"

"Just one right now," she says. "Unit four. Januarys are always slow. Was there anyone else in the car?"

"No. Did you think there was?"

"I wasn't sure."

She feels a sudden shiver, hugs herself. A small portable heater hums in one corner, but the office is still cold. Her lower back aches. She pulled something dragging the man into the lot.

The flatbed backs and fills, the reverse alarm beeping. Where the car was, the roadway is scorched dark.

"How do you stay in business?" he says. "Renting one out of ten?"

"It's not my motel. I'm just the day manager. Four days a week."

The flatbed drives off.

"What time did you come in?"

"Ten."

"Till when?"

"Ten tonight."

"That's a long shift."

"A few things I need to do, but mostly I end up watching a lot of TV."

"Any cameras outside? Video?"

"No."

"And no other witnesses you know of?"

"I was the only one here."

"No maid? Maintenance guy?"

"This time of year, I only call them when I need them."

"So you're alone most of the time?"

"Yes."

She can still smell smoke and burned rubber, knows it's on her clothes, her skin.

The door chime sounds, and another trooper comes in. She's younger than Joette, hair tied up under a blue-and-yellow peaked cap. The silver name tag on her uniform reads LT. BRYCE.

"How long you been working here?" Chaney says.

"A year and a half," Joette says. "Before that, I was at First Community in Belmar." Not sure why she felt the need to tell him.

"The bank?" he says. "What did you do there?"

"I was a teller."

"You quit?"

"They got bought. I got downsized."

"I hear that. You get a pension at least?"

She shakes her head.

"That your car out there?" Bryce says.

"Yes."

Bryce looks around the office, Joette aware of what she must be seeing. Cheap paneling, a rack of sun-faded tourist brochures. The green indoor-outdoor carpet has water stains left over from Hurricane Sandy in 2012. Knowing Singh, she assumed he'd put in for FEMA money after the storm, but he never made any repairs.

Bryce nods at the curtained doorway that leads to the back room. "What's in there?"

"Filing cabinet. Breaker box, supplies. Stock for the vending machines. Fire exit."

"This some kind of welfare motel?"

"Excuse me?"

"Section Eight placement? Social Services?"

"No."

"Usually, when we roll up on a place like this, we're kicking in doors."

Joette feels a flash of irritation, says nothing.

"How come you didn't call 911 right away?" Bryce says. "Why go out there on your own?"

"It seemed like the right thing to do. I didn't think too much about it."

"Don't you know you're not supposed to move accident victims?"

"The car was on fire," she says. "If I hadn't pulled him out, he would have burned to death."

"Why are you getting agitated?"

"I'm not agitated. You asked me a question. I answered it."

Chaney gets up, closes his notebook. "Different here in the summer, I imagine, once all the bennies come down."

"We're full up Memorial Day to Labor Day. We're only fifteen minutes from the beach."

"More like a half hour," Bryce says. "How much you get for a room?"

"You interested?" Feeling defensive now. *Shut up. Let them leave.*

"Hardly," Bryce says.

"Depends on length of stay. Different rates on- and off-season. The rooms are all efficiencies, so mostly we rent weekly or monthly. We get a lot of people stay all summer. Families."

"If you say so."

It's getting dark outside. She'll have to switch on the road-side sign soon. Doesn't want to. She just wants to close up and go home.

Another Wall cruiser pulls into the lot, Noah Cooper at the wheel. A familiar face at last. He gets out, looks toward the office, then goes over to talk to the other uniforms.

"You sure you don't want to go to the ER?" Chaney says. "Get that arm looked at?"

"No. I'll be fine."

"You might think different later, when it starts hurting."

"It hurts now. But thanks."

Noah comes in, the door chiming. He nods to the troopers, looks at her. "You all right?"

"You two know each other?" Bryce says.

"Yeah," Noah says before Joette can answer. "Long time."

"We're out of here," Chaney says. He looks at Bryce. "Unless you got something else."

Bryce shakes her head. They nod to Noah as they leave. Joette watches Bryce go to her Subaru, bend to look into the passenger-side window. She feels her stomach tighten.

Bryce straightens, says something to Chaney. He shrugs and they get into their cruisers, pull out of the lot. The other cops drift to their cars and drive off, no lights or sirens this time.

"You're hurt," Noah says.

"It's not bad. Little surface burn is all."

"They told me what happened. You really pull the driver out of that car?"

"I'm as surprised as you are."

"That's some superhero stuff."

"He didn't make it."

"I heard. I'm sorry."

Almost full dark now. In the back room, she opens the

breaker box and thumbs switches. When she comes back out, the neon sign is flickering. It buzzes and hums, then finally lights up—CASTAWAYS MOT R LODGE—CABLE TV—BEST RATES—VACANCY. The second O in MOTOR stays dark, as always. The sign throws a red glow on the parking lot, Noah's cruiser and her Subaru.

She picks grit from her palm from when she fell. All of it settling in on her now. What happened, what she did.

"Anyone else see the accident?" he says.

"Just me, far as I know."

"What about stripper mom?"

"Don't call her that."

"Sorry. Brianna."

"She wasn't here. Cara either. They've been gone all day."

"That's good. Not something you'd want a kid to see, an accident like that. Give her nightmares."

Flecks of snow outside now. She remembers the ash.

"What about you?" he says.

"What about me?"

"Will you have nightmares?"

"I have enough already," she says. "Any new ones will have to wait in line."

———

After he's gone, she calls Singh at his house in Edison to tell him about the accident. All he wants to know is if there's any damage to motel property, if they'll have any liability for the driver dying there. He doesn't ask if she wants Baxter, the night man, to come in early.

She's anxious, knowing what she has to do. She watches the office clock while the TV drones on the wall. A little after seven, the wind picks up, and she knows she can't wait any longer. She pulls on her hoodie and down vest, gets the heavy black aluminum flashlight from the back room.

Outside, the snow is still light. She sees a lone car coming down the highway, waits for it to pass. Then she crosses to the opposite shoulder, turns on the flashlight. The beam lights bits of safety glass that were swept off the road. The slope leads down to a rain ditch on the edge of the woods.

You have to make sure.

She shines the light in the ditch, picks her way down carefully, playing the beam along the ground, then into the trees. There are shards of black plastic scattered around, pieces of the car's front end. She walks the ditch toward the creek and bridge, doing grids with the flashlight beam, taking her time. Easier to search in the daylight, but she can't come back then, take the chance of being seen.

She hears a car engine, shuts off the flashlight. Headlights coming fast. The car flies by above her, makes the metal bridge surface hum. When the taillights are out of sight, she turns on the flashlight again.

The water in the creek is only a few inches deep but slivered with ice. She fans the beam under the bridge and into the culvert. Trash has washed up on the concrete ledge—a sodden red-and-white KFC box, a plastic Diet Coke bottle. Just below the surface, something dark and rectangular is caught on a dead branch.

She steps into the creek, cold water filling her sneakers, tucks the flashlight under her left arm. She pushes up her other sleeve, shines the flashlight into the water. There it is, trailing from the branch. Another bill.

She reaches in, the coldness of the water numbing her hand, frees the bill and shines the light on it. Another hundred, one corner burned off. The loose bills must have been caught in the updraft of heat from the fire, floated clear of the trunk. Are there more?

She tucks the bill in a vest pocket, ducks under the culvert and steps onto the narrow concrete ledge of the creek bank, her sneakers squishing. Walking heel to toe on the ledge, she sweeps the flashlight beam side to side. At the end of the culvert, she steps to the other bank, walks back that way, ducking low again. Slower this time, doing grids again with the flashlight. No more bills.

Back to the ditch, then up to the road, her feet soaked and numb. In the office, she takes off her sneakers and socks, rolls up her jeans cuffs midcalf. She lays the wet socks over the heater grille, sets the sneakers in front of it. The floor is cold beneath her bare feet. She dries them with a towel from the back room linen closet.

She smooths out the wet bill on the desk, the half-burned one beside it. There may be more around, blown down the road or into the woods, but there's nothing she can do about that now.

She holds the bills up to the light. They're real as far as she can tell, the blue security ribbons intact. To the left of Franklin are the embedded threads that read USA and 100.

A sudden chill sweeps through her again, goose bumps from the cold. The pain in her back has returned.

At nine, the door locks automatically with a sharp click that startles her. At ten-thirty, Baxter's beat-up station wagon pulls into the lot. She tucks the bills in her vest pocket, buzzes him in. He's carrying a grease-soaked White Castle bag, has the smell of alcohol on his breath.

"Didn't have time for dinner," he says. He raises the hinged wooden flap at the end of the counter. "Had to grab something on the way. Want a slider?"

"Ugh. No thanks."

Her socks are dry now, warm from the heater. She starts to pull them on, sees he's looking at the tattoo above her right ankle, the blue rose and the spiral of thorns that circle her calf. She pulls up her sock to cover it, slips on her still-damp sneakers.

She tells him about the accident, but his attention drifts, and there's a loss of focus in his eyes. He takes the remote from the counter, starts flipping channels. He'll be asleep at the desk by eleven.

Outside in the cold, clouds hide the moon. She resists the temptation to open the Subaru's trunk, look inside. Baxter might be watching.

She starts the engine, turns up the heat, grips the wheel.

Drive away now, and everything's different. You're different.

Three deep breaths. She looks back toward the office. Sure enough, Baxter's at the window.

She backs up and steers around his station wagon. Snow flurries shine in her headlights. She turns on the wipers, pulls out of the neon-lit lot and onto the dark highway.

THREE

THE MOTION-SENSOR light over the trailer door switches on as she pulls into the carport. Home. She shuts off the engine and headlights. It's quiet, except for the sound of a TV in the double-wide next door. Her trailer's at the end of the row, an empty lot on the other side.

You can't just sit here.

She's light-headed as she goes up the wooden steps and unlocks the trailer door. A single lamp is on in the living room. The rest of the trailer is dark, the curtains closed. It's cold. She set the thermostat to sixty, as she always does when she leaves in the morning, trying to keep the heating bill down. Now she raises it to sixty-eight, hears the heat kick on. A dusty smell rises from the floor vents.

The carport light goes out. From the kitchenette

window, she can see up the road to the park entrance. No one following her. No police cars. No flashing lights. No sirens.

Eleven-fifteen by her watch. She'll wait. The trailers around her will be dark by midnight. Normal people with normal jobs. No one staying up late, spying on their neighbors.

There are three bottles of Blue Moon left in the refrigerator. She opens one, doesn't bother with a glass. She takes it into the living room, sits on the couch and turns off the lamp. She feels safe now, calmer than she's been in hours.

Halfway through the beer, she already has a slight buzz. When the bottle's empty, she considers getting another. She closes her eyes, drifts, then is suddenly awake again.

She looks at her watch. One a.m. Almost two hours gone.

At the window, she parts the blinds, looks out at the Subaru. She switches off the motion sensor so it won't activate, then puts on her hoodie again, goes outside.

No more snow. The sky is clear, with a bow around the moon. The TV's off in the trailer next door, the windows dark. She can hear the hum of cars out on Route 35.

When she opens the trunk, the inside bulb lights up the sheet she took from the motel's linen closet. Under it is the gear bag, canvas sides browned by heat.

It's heavier than she remembered. She closes the trunk, carries the bag inside, locks and chains the front door. In the bedroom, she turns on the overhead light, slides the door shut behind her. She sets the bag on the low bed, unzips it and looks at the money inside.

Take your time. Be careful.

She goes through the strapped bills, looking for dye packs, GPS trackers. But she already knows this isn't bank money. The paper straps are generic—no bank name, logo or denominations. There's a torn strap and more loose bills at the bottom of the bag. All hundreds.

She lines the packs up on the comforter in three rows. Most of the packs are hundreds, the rest fifties. She wipes wet palms on her jeans.

Stop stalling. Count it.

The hundreds are in standard $10,000 packs, the fifties in packs of $5,000. Some of the bills are soiled, creased. None of the serial numbers are in sequence.

She gets the Dri Mark pen from her dresser, draws an amber line across one of the hundreds. It fades quickly. If the bill were counterfeit, the line would show black, the ink reacting to the quality of the paper. She marks other bills from different packs. An amber line each time, fading to nothing.

She counts ninety-eight loose hundreds, binds them with a rubber band, feels a sense of relief. The two damaged bills complete that pack. That means there might not be any others blowing around out there on the road or in the woods, waiting for someone to find them.

It takes her three tries to count it all, losing track and coming up with a different total each time. Finally she gets her phone, uses the calculator app, typing in numbers as she counts again.

With the two damaged bills figured in, the total comes to $250,000 in hundreds, another $50,000 in fifties. She's looking at $299,800 spread out on the bed.

She sits back, has to put a hand against the dresser to keep from falling.

Get it out of here. Take it back.

But where? And to who?

If she hadn't grabbed the bag when she did, if she'd

hesitated even a few more minutes, the money would have caught fire, gone up with the rest of the car. And the driver—maybe the only one who knew it was there—is dead. If anyone else is looking for the money, they might assume it was destroyed in the fire. Maybe now it belongs to no one at all. Except her.

She gets her roll-on suitcase from the closet, opens it on the floor and stacks the money inside. Three pairs of jeans go over the bills to keep them in place. She zips the suitcase shut and sets it back in the closet, upright against the wall behind her hanging clothes.

It all hits her then, and she can't trust her legs. She sits on the bed, looks at the suitcase half hidden in the closet. She's still cold, and the burn on her arm is stinging again. Wind whines around the trailer, a hollow, lonesome sound. She wants another beer, but first she needs to get rid of the gear bag.

The other trailers are still dark. She puts the bag in the Subaru's trunk, starts the engine. At the park exit, she turns south on Route 35. She takes it to the Asbury circle, then heads west.

In twenty minutes, she's on the outskirts of Freehold. She spots an open dumpster behind a dark supermarket, pulls up alongside it and kills her lights, leaves the engine running. Cars pass by, but no one slows.

Do it quick.

She gets the bag from the trunk, checks it one last time to make sure it's empty, then tosses it up and into the dumpster.

Driving back, she listens to a local station playing classic rock. When the hourly news comes on, she turns up the volume, but there's nothing about the accident.

Her arm is sore and throbbing beneath the bandage. Back

in the trailer, tired now, she opens another Blue Moon, washes down two ibuprofen.

She checks the window and door locks, takes the bottle into the living room. Then she sits in the dark and listens to the wind.

FOUR

HELEN'S WAITING AT the diner in their regular booth by the window. It's just before eight, the morning cold and clear. The diner's crowded, loud with voices and the clinking of silverware and glass.

Joette woke with a headache and a dry mouth. She lay in bed staring at the ceiling, thinking about the suitcase, tempted to take it out, look at the money inside. Proof it wasn't all a dream.

"Ouch," Helen says. "Rough night?"

Joette slides into the booth. She's put on a long-sleeved black T-shirt to hide the bandage on her arm. She knows the way she looks—puffy eyes, dark circles. "Not sleeping so well these days."

"You're losing more weight too," Helen says. "What's up with that?"

"Not much appetite." She's dropped ten pounds in the last two months without trying, her jeans riding low and slack.

"You're not sick, are you?"

"Just nerves."

She wants to tell Helen about the accident, but that would take too long, raise too many questions she doesn't want to answer.

"From what?" Helen says. "Worried about your meeting?"

"They are what they are. It's never good news."

"What's this one about?"

"Same as usual, I expect. Where I'm at with the Medicaid application. An update on how she's doing. Which these days is always the same, or worse."

When the waitress comes over, Joette orders coffee and rye toast, Helen an omelet.

"Her house is up for sale, so there's nothing more I can do with it," Joette says. "If the market changes, it might sell, but I can't count on that. We're doing private pay until her assets are zeroed out. At nine grand a month, that won't be long. Medicaid keeps asking for more paperwork in the meantime—receipts, tax returns. Stuff I don't think she even kept."

"Aren't there lawyers you can hire for that, help the process along?"

"Three-grand retainer to start with, ones I talked to."

"What about her will?"

"I'm the executor, but there isn't much to the estate. Just the house and whatever cash might be left, which at that point will likely be none."

"I don't know how you do it," Helen says. "Handling all this on your own."

"Wasn't much choice."

"I know, but still. It must seem overwhelming at times."

"When are you going in?"

"Ten. Probably be on drive-through until close. Half the people in the office are sick, with whatever it is that's going around. Everybody's worried it's the virus again. Lots of hacking and coughing. Good times."

"Why don't they stay home?"

"It's different since the sale. No sick days anymore. Just PTO—Personal Time Off. You get seven days a year. If you miss a day because you're sick, it comes out of those."

"What if you're sick more than seven days?"

"Then you have to use your vacation time. Or go on short-term medical leave. Which no one wants to do, because they might not have a job when they get back."

"That doesn't sound legal," Joette says. "Surprised someone hasn't gone after them on that."

"That's the least of their worries. Word is a judgment's coming soon on this latest consumer protection case. Probably a big fine, and some more middle managers thrown under the bus. In the meantime, corporate's handing out seven-figure bonuses and pension packages to board members as fast as it can. Rats, meet ship."

The waitress brings their food. Joette takes a bite of toast, realizes she isn't hungry. "I miss it sometimes, the bank. Miss the people mostly."

"Don't. It's not the way you remember it. There's been so much turnover you wouldn't know most of the people there anyway. The place you remember is gone."

"It was a good job, compared to some I've had. Lasted the longest, too. Always thought I was lucky to get it, especially with nothing but a GED and two years at Brookdale. I didn't want to leave."

"I'm sorry the way that worked out," Helen says. "It wasn't fair."

"What is?"

Joette reaches for the glass sugar canister, knocks it over. A trail of crystals spills on the table.

"You *are* nervous," Helen says.

Joette rights the canister, shakes sugar into her coffee, sweeps the spilled crystals under the saucer.

"Try a real breakfast someday," Helen says. "Eggs at least, get some protein into you. You look like you could use it."

Her hand's unsteady as she picks up the cup.

"How are things at the motel?" Helen says.

"Same. I think Singh's just waiting to hear the right numbers from a developer so he can sell the property. Way he sees it, why bother fixing anything in the meantime? Or I guess he could just torch the place for the insurance, if he still has any. You gonna stay on there at the bank?"

"Long as I can. If they fire me, they fire me, but I'm not quitting. Not with Leona at Howard, and Curtis headed there next year. And Leona's got her heart set on law school afterward. How we're going to make that happen, I don't know."

"You must be proud of them."

"I am. Every day. But I envy you sometimes."

"Why would you possibly do that?"

"Your freedom. Being able to do anything you want."

"It's not the way it looks. I still have to work. I still have debts."

"But you could leave if you wanted to, when the situation with your mother changes. You could pick up, go somewhere else. Start over again."

"You mean when she dies?"

"I know you've thought about it. You're still young."

"I'll be forty in two months."

"Young enough. There's nothing else holding you here.

You've done everything you needed to, everything you should have. Made every decision, paid every bill. You've been a good daughter. The best."

Joette feels water come to her eyes, looks away.

"I worry about you, Jo. You've been through hell, dealt with more than most people ever have to in their lives. Troy getting sick. Your mom's stroke."

"People deal with worse."

"We're not talking about other people, are we? We're talking about you."

Joette's thumb finds her left wrist, rubs the raised scars there. She has to will herself to stop. "Don't worry about me."

"Stoic as always. You never change. Your mom was the same way. Tough lady when she had to be."

"Can't blame her. She had her hands full with me after my father died. She put up with a lot, all the trouble I got into."

"Come on, you weren't that bad, were you?"

"I ran away a couple times. Got as far as Wildwood once. Don't know what I thought I was doing."

"How old were you?"

"Fifteen. I'd been acting out for a couple years already, I'm sure. Stupid things. Kid things."

"Why Wildwood?"

"We'd been there once, at an amusement park, when my father was alive."

"You never told me this."

"Yeah, fifteen years old and dumb as a rock, hitchhiking in the summer. Slept on the beach that night. Wildwood cops found me the next day, called my mother. She had to come down and get me. She wasn't happy."

"Good thing they did. Who knows where you would have

ended up. If one of my kids had done that, I would have grounded them until they were thirty."

They eat in silence. The toast is limp and tasteless. She can only finish one slice.

"Hang in there," Helen says. "It's about time for your luck to turn around anyway, isn't it?"

"You believe that?"

"Why not? You're due."

She thinks about the money again, the glowing bill dancing in front of her, waiting to be plucked from the air.

"Maybe I am," she says.

FIVE

——

SHE PARKS IN the visitors' lot at the nursing home, signs in at the security desk. Annalisa, the social worker, is waiting for her in the lobby. Together they walk down to the conference room. Lourdes, the head of nursing, and Nora from the billing office are already there, files open in front of them.

Joette hates this room, the still lifes on the walls, the long polished-wood table. Nothing good happens here.

"Thanks so much for coming, Jo," Lourdes says. "Have you been up to see your mom yet?"

Joette sits across from her. "No. I will when we're done."

At the head of the table, Annalisa says, "Who wants to start?"

Lourdes gives Joette a smile. "I'll jump right in then. Your mother was evaluated again this week, at my request.

I wanted to make sure I had the most recent results for our meeting. She's on a pureed diet now, as you know."

"I've fed her. Is that the way it'll be from now on? Baby food?"

"It's for her safety. The issue is her swallowing reflex, which is getting weaker. It might be that something changes going forward and we see an improvement, but it's unlikely. I'd be giving you false hope to tell you different."

"I've spent a lot of time with her this week," Annalisa says. "Most of the day she's in the activity room. She does well there. She watches TV, and we have music twice a week. She seems to enjoy that."

"How do we know? She can't even speak."

Ease up, Joette thinks. *They're only trying to help.*

"Watching a loved one decline is always upsetting," Annalisa says. "But we're doing everything we can to keep her as comfortable as possible. That's all we can do at this stage."

Joette feels the tears coming, blinks them back. "And when she can't swallow at all anymore?"

"Then we may have some difficult choices to make," Annalisa says.

"You mean I will."

"As her daughter and Power of Attorney, yes. I know she has an advance directive on file."

"And a DNR," Joette says. "And by choices, you mean a feeding tube."

"Some families choose to do that."

"At that point, her directive kicks in anyway, doesn't it? 'No heroic measures'?"

Lourdes takes a box of tissues from the credenza behind her, sets it on the table.

"Your mother entrusted you to make those decisions for her, as her POA," Annalisa says. "And that's what you've done. There's no sense in second-guessing yourself."

"I've second-guessed every decision I've made in the past two years."

"It can feel that way sometimes," Annalisa says. "I know. Either way, the consensus is we'll be looking at a palliative care option soon."

"You mean hospice?"

"Lourdes?" Annalisa says.

"Hospice care doesn't always mean death is imminent," Lourdes says. "It just allows us to have extra aides here to spend time with your mom. A lot of families find it lets them take a breather from visiting every day, relieves some of the burden."

"And that means no more medical care?"

"For the most part, yes," Annalisa says. "That's a prerequisite for hospice. But as I say, it's a decision only you can make. And you don't have to make it today."

"Before her stroke, my mother was very clear about what she would want—and not want—if something like this ever happened to her. I've tried to respect her wishes."

"We understand."

Nora speaks for the first time. "I hate to bring this up now, but there's something else we need to address."

Here it comes.

"I went over your Medicaid paperwork again this morning. It's still pending, as you know."

"Her house is on the market," Joette says. "I cleaned it out, sold all the furniture that was worth selling. I've dropped the asking price twice. There's nothing more I can do. When it sells, it sells."

"Another option is to sign it over to us now," Nora says. "Then you don't need to worry about it anymore. We'll take care of the rest."

"I don't know if I want to do that."

"It's something worth keeping in mind. It might take some of the stress off you."

"Another thing to consider," Annalisa says. "Despite everything she's been through, your mom's pretty resilient. Even in hospice, she could go on this way for months."

"She wouldn't want that," Joette says. "And she wouldn't want to be the way she is now."

"That's why the burden, unfair as it may seem, falls to you again," Annalisa says. "With no other immediate family, no siblings you've told us about..."

"There are none. It's just me."

Lourdes reaches out and lays a hand over hers.

Nora says, "The problem, as we talked about at our last meeting, is if you run out of funds while your mother is still alive. Then we may be in a situation where we have to consider placing her in a different facility, one that's a better fit for her financial resources."

"She's been here two years now," Joette says. "She's used to it."

"We're all hoping it doesn't come to that," Nora says. "But to be honest, if we did relocate her, she might not even be aware of it."

"You don't know that," Joette says.

Nora sits back. No one speaks.

Joette looks at the tissues, wants to take one. Doesn't.

"I'll deal with it all," she says. "Whatever it takes."

———

The third-floor activity room is full of light. Her mother is sleeping in a hospital Geri chair near the big windows, bundled in a blanket despite the room's close heat.

Alora, one of the Haitian aides, is opening containers of pudding at a table. Beside her, a woman in a wheelchair clutches a cloth doll, kneading it in bony hands. She has thinning gray hair and lost, watery eyes, as if she's about to cry.

"Miss Joette." Alora smiles. "How are you this morning?"

Four other residents, all women, are in wheelchairs in front of a big television showing *The Wizard of Oz*. Everyone else is still at breakfast, Joette guesses, or already in physical therapy.

"Miss Irene is sleepy today," Alora says. "I tried to feed her, but she wouldn't eat."

Joette crouches beside her mother's chair. Beneath the blanket, her right leg is bent under her left, the muscles constricted. What's left of her silver hair is combed neatly, pink scalp showing through. She smells of soap.

"Hi, Mom."

No response at first, then her eyes open. Joette puts a hand on the blanket, over the jutting shape of her mother's knee. Even through the material, she feels the sharp edges of bone, the skin there paper-thin. Her mother turns to her without expression. The faintest of smiles, then her glance passes over her to the wall beyond.

Joette leans close, kisses her cheek. "It's me, Mom."

Alora comes up behind them. "Maybe she'd like some of this." She's holding a container of chocolate pudding wrapped in a napkin, a white plastic spoon stuck in it.

Joette wipes her eyes with the back of her wrist. "Yes, thank you."

She takes the cup, spoons up pudding, holds it in front

of her mother's face. Her mother looks at it, then opens her mouth slightly, almost a reflex, closes it over the spoon. When Joette draws it out, it's clear of pudding. She remembers what Lourdes said, watches her mother's throat work as she swallows.

Five spoonfuls and the pudding's almost gone. Joette scrapes out the last of it, then uses the napkin to wipe her mother's lips.

Alora puts a hand on Joette's shoulder, squeezes gently, takes the container and spoon.

Joette's mother gives her a last look, no recognition in her eyes, then turns toward the TV, the flickering images there.

"I'm gonna go now, Mom. But I'll be back before you know it." She kisses her mother's forehead. "I love you."

Her mother's eyes slowly close. She's asleep again.

At the door, Alora hugs her. The woman with the doll watches them.

She keeps it together on her way out of the building. Once in the car, the fear hits her, as it always does when she leaves. That maybe this is the last time. That she'll never see her mother alive again.

There's no holding back then. She begins to cry, alone in the cold morning sun.

———

On the way to the motel, she stops at a Wawa, buys their last *Asbury Park Press*, pages through it in the car.

The accident only gets three paragraphs on page four— *Motorist dies in fiery crash*. It's a bare-bones press release. No photo.

The last paragraph reads: *The driver, Thomas Nash, a*

Barnegat resident, was pronounced dead at the scene. State police are investigating.

The story gives the accident location but doesn't name the motel. No mention of the driver's injuries, no mention of her.

Nothing about the money.

SIX

HE FUCKED US," Cosmo says. "I didn't think he had it in him, but he did. He fucked us."

"We don't know that," Travis says. "We don't know anything yet."

They're in Cosmo's new Lexus SUV, parked in the NJ Transit commuter lot in Middletown, engine running for warmth. Sleet clicks on the roof. Four in the afternoon, and it's already dark. Cars idle near the elevated platform, lights on, exhaust showing in the cold air. Travis's Chevy Silverado 1500 is parked a few spots away under a light pole.

"Not many ways it could have gone," Cosmo says. "He took us off, and they did the same to him. They've got our money."

"Maybe." He's been running it through his head all day, how it might have played out.

"Only way it reads," Cosmo says. "He tried to do the deal without us. We shouldn't have trusted him, let him hold that cash."

"Wasn't a problem before. No reason to think it would be this time."

"You know what bothers me most? He thought he'd get away with it. That we'd just lay there and take a fucking like that."

Travis rubs his two-day beard, looks out the window at the acres of parked cars.

"Sorry. He was your guy," Cosmo says.

Travis turns to him. "Meaning what?"

"The two of you went back, right?"

Travis meets his eyes until Cosmo has to look away.

"He was your friend, I know," Cosmo says. Choosing his words carefully now. "It hurts when you think you know someone, turns out you don't."

A train horn sounds. Barrier arms swing down across the roadway, red lights flashing. A southbound train slows as it draws into the station, brakes squealing, then jerks to a halt. The doors thunk open, and people spill out onto the platform, popping umbrellas. Horns beep from waiting cars.

Look at them all, Travis thinks. *The same routine every day. And for what?*

"He was a guy I knew from the yard," he says. "That's all. I kept him from getting his wig split once. We were both out a couple years before I saw him again. He came to me with the Dominican deal. It sounded good. Sounded good to you, too."

"It did, until now. All this time, no beefs, everybody earning. Should have known it was too sweet to last. Either way, we lost our plug."

"Maybe not," Travis says. "I'll go up there tonight, talk to them."

"You serious? For Christ's sake, they shot him. How do you think they're gonna react to you?"

"I want to hear what they have to say."

"You think they're just gonna let you walk out of there?"

The doors close, and the train moves off. The barrier arms rise again. Cars begin to file out of the lot.

"I'll take my chances with the Ds," Travis says. "You start looking for another connect. We go dry too long, our people will start buying from someone else, and we won't get them back. See if anyone's holding product they want to move fast. What did the story in the paper say?"

"Not much. I got most of the details from my guy at the state police. I reached out to him after I heard it on the radio."

"Since when are you tight with the state cops?"

"Just this one. He's useful. I slip him a few bucks now and then, he lets me know what's going down, who's on the radar for a bust. He's the one told me Tommy was shot. It wasn't in the paper."

"He ask why you were interested?"

"No. He knows better than that. Told me Tommy was definitely heading south when he crashed though. Probably trying to get to a hospital. If he hadn't wrecked, he might have made it, still be alive. And we'd know where our money was."

"If he had it."

"I'm betting he did," Cosmo says. "I called him twice yesterday, work out some details on the next meet. No answer. I went by his place. Nobody there, and his BMW's gone. Couple hours later, I heard the news. Then I called you."

"What are the chances your trooper friend or his buddies found the money after the crash, helped themselves?"

"Unlikely. My guy wasn't there, but he talked to the troopers who were. They said there wasn't much left of the car when they arrived. Probably had a full tank of gas, why it burned so fast. Also, there was a woman saw the accident, was there the whole time."

"What woman?"

"At the motel near where it happened. She pulled Tommy out of the car before it blew."

"He was alive?"

"Yeah, survived the crash. It was the bullet killed him. You sure you want to go up there, deal with those people?"

"Whether they took him off or not, they'll assume we think they did. They'll be waiting for us to come at them. Or they might decide to come at us first. Preemptive strike."

"Outstanding."

"I need to know where we are with them. Better to find out now."

Cosmo shakes his head. "That fucking Tommy. A setup like this, serious money, minimal risk. And he had to get greedy."

"It happens," Travis says.

SEVEN

TRAVIS STANDS BENEATH a sign that reads TIRES NEW AND USED, knocks on a side door. It's an industrial block in Newark, close enough to the Turnpike that he can hear traffic noise.

No rain now, but the air is cold and damp. An airliner comes in low out of the overcast, landing lights flashing. It seems to hang suspended in the air as it nears the airport, less than a mile away. The howl of its engines echoes between the buildings.

Locks scrape, and the door is opened by a dark-skinned man he's never seen before. He has wide shoulders and dreadlocks, wears a long duster, his right hand in the pocket. Another of Chano's Dominicans. Extra muscle.

He gestures Travis inside, locks and bolts the door behind him.

Two lift bays, piles of used tires. New ones, still stickered, are in a rack against the wall. On the far side, the windows of an elevated office throw light on the shop floor. Chano and the Rejas brothers, Jorge and Aldo, stand behind the glass, looking down at him.

The dreadlocked man raises his chin in the direction of the office. Travis crosses the bays, goes up the short flight of wooden steps. The office door is ajar, an old-fashioned brown shade pulled down over the glass.

The brothers move to opposite sides of the room as he comes in. Jorge's head is shaven, Aldo has a ponytail—the only way Travis can tell them apart. They both wear long sleeveless jerseys.

Chano sits down behind a metal desk, the brothers flanking him. There's a 9mm automatic on the desktop. Next to it, a photo in a silver frame. Chano sitting at a picnic table, smiling, a dark-haired toddler on his lap.

Travis nods at the gun. "That necessary?"

The dreadlocked man comes up the stairs behind him.

"Have to be careful, *papi*," Chano says. "These are uncertain times."

"They are."

Chano is older than the brothers, his hair and neat beard streaked with gray. There's a faded blue tattoo on the side of his neck. "You alone?"

"Like I said I'd be." Cosmo is in the Lexus, parked five blocks away, waiting for Travis's call. If it doesn't come in an hour, he'll know things have gone bad. He'll go home, pack, run.

Travis takes off his jacket, drapes it on a metal chair, raises his arms, ready to be searched.

"This time I think you need to show us some skin, homes," Chano says.

"Show you more than that." He lifts his T-shirt to expose

the nylon money belt. He peels the Velcro loose, coils the belt and sets it on the desk. Then he pulls the T-shirt off over his head, turns slowly.

"Goddamn," Aldo says. They're looking at his scars.

He faces Chano again, drops the T-shirt on the chair, starts to tug at his belt buckle.

"Nah, that's good. Sorry, *papi*. Got to do it. Been enough drama already."

Chano speaks Spanish to the dreadlocked man. He leaves the office, shuts the door and goes down the steps to the shop floor.

Travis puts his T-shirt back on.

"Respect for coming here," Chano says. "I was worried you might have got the wrong idea about some things."

"That your grandson in the photo?" he says.

"My daughter's boy. He just turned four. Looks like me, no?"

"I see it."

"What's in the belt?"

"Ten grand."

"For what?"

"For you. A good-faith gesture. So there are no misunderstandings."

Chano opens a drawer, puts the gun inside, but doesn't close it. "Glad to hear you say that. You did the right thing, calling. Sorry about your boy Tommy. But you need to hear it from me, how it went down."

"Why I came."

"He called a couple days ago, said he was ready to do the pickup. Little earlier than we expected, but we put the package together, same as always. We been switching it up lately, so I told him to come to JC, a detail place my brother-in-law owns. You been there."

"I remember it."

"He wanted to do it in the afternoon, before they closed. Maybe he didn't trust us, wanted other people around, I don't know. I didn't like it. Little bit of an insult, you know? And you not being there, that didn't feel right."

"What time?"

"Maybe four o'clock?" He looks at Aldo, who nods.

"He had the money with him?"

"In a bag, like you bring to the gym," Chano says. "He was nervous as shit, too. He hands it over, and Aldo takes out the cash, starts counting. I say, 'Where's my man, Travis? Why isn't he here?' He says you sent him. I didn't believe him. The money was right, though...."

"How much?"

"Same as last time. Three hundred for four keys. Jorge brings it out, metal case, packed right, and your boy pulls a piece. Tells Aldo to put the money back in the bag, wants Jorge to hand over the case. Some *cojones*, right? I say 'Fuck that, no way that shit leaves here.' Whole time, though, he's waving that gun around, acting janky, like he's gonna start popping off any minute. I wasn't even carrying. Aldo was, though."

"How did it play?"

"I tell your boy shoot us or get the fuck out—that case ain't going nowhere. I think for a minute there, he was gonna do it. His finger's on the trigger. I can see it."

"What type of weapon?"

"Aldo, what was it?"

"Glock nine."

Travis remembers the gun. Tommy showed it to him.

"Aldo pulls his own nine, then it gets crazy in there. Your boy lets off a couple, but he misses. Ricochet goes right by my head. Aldo didn't miss."

"Where was he hit?"

"Stomach, I think. Drops his gun, grabs the bag with the money, runs out the door."

"You let him go?"

"Too public. Bad enough that shit's happening middle of the afternoon. Aldo wanted to go after him, but I said, 'Let him go his way.' We had to shut the place down, turn off all the lights. Thought somebody might have heard the shots, called the police."

"All that money and you let him walk?"

"More trouble than it was worth. I just wanted him the fuck gone."

"What did you do with his gun?"

"In the river. Had to do Aldo's piece the same way. Your boy put us through a lot of stress and anxiety, man. Very unprofessional. We were all a little upset by it, no joke."

"He's dead."

"That's too bad. But he brought it on himself."

"He did."

Travis can picture it. Tommy coming on hard, a gun in his hand, then panicking as things went bad.

"You were right about the money," he says. "He was holding it until we set up the next exchange. He decided to try to swing the deal himself."

"That's some in-house shit. Your problem. Not ours."

"I agree," Travis says. "So where's that leave us?"

"Leaves *me* thinking we should chill on this for a while, reevaluate our relationship."

"We still want what you got. I just need a few days, get the money together."

"What happened to the cash your boy was carrying?"

"I don't know."

Chano sits back, strokes his beard. "You think we took it?"

"Didn't say that."

"Would have been justified if we did, way he acted."

"You would have been."

Chano smiles. "You white boys think we need you, because you can sell to people down there won't buy from us. But you're small-time without us, homes. We both know that. I knew it the first time your boy came to me, wanted to hook up."

"Didn't stop you from saying yes. You made some good money with us."

"We did. But I knew it wouldn't last. Some people, they get a good thing going, and they can't help but fuck it up. It's their nature."

"That's why I'm here. Get things running smoothly again."

"Get it straight, though, man. You need us, but we don't need you. Everybody wants what we got. Buyers get in line because our shit comes pure, from China. I'm talking about people that do business in a calm and reasonable manner. They can't get enough. I could sell your package tomorrow for twice what you were paying. Why put up with this hassle?"

"No hassle. Two years without an issue between us. Tommy made a mistake. He's gone. No need to let that disrupt our arrangement."

"Your boy already disrupted it. And if we do business again, I think that price needs to go up. For our trouble."

He wondered how long it would take to get to that, knew it was coming.

"That's what the ten's for," he says. "Smooth things over."

"Ten, man. Ten's nothing."

"That's above and beyond what we'll go for the next package. We agree on a price, I'll let you know when the money's together. You want to do the deal then, we'll do it.

You don't, we both walk away and leave it at that. You keep the ten for your trouble."

To Aldo, Chano says, "Check that." Then to Travis. "No offense."

"None taken."

Aldo takes the single pack of hundreds from the belt, counts the bills.

"Only reason we're even talking is because I respect you," Chano says. "And the business we've done together."

"I know," Travis says.

"*Es bueno,*" Aldo says. He puts the money back in the belt.

"Right now I need to take a leak," Travis says. "Had a long drive up in traffic. Bumper-to-bumper on Seventy-Eight."

Chano looks at him for a moment, then points to an open door at the back of the office. Travis goes around the desk and into a narrow bathroom. A string brushes his face. He pulls it to turn on the overhead bulb, illuminating a single toilet and a small sink. Graffiti on the walls. The smell of urine and cleaning fluid.

The door closes on its spring behind him. He props a work boot on the toilet seat, draws up his right jeans leg and pulls loose the little Ruger .380 taped above his inside ankle. He eases back the slide to make sure there's a round chambered, then flushes the tape down the toilet, his foot on the lever.

Through the door, he hears them speaking Spanish, voices low. He tries to picture where they are in the room.

Another plane approaches. He waits for the rumbling to grow louder. When it's directly overhead, he shoulders open the door.

Jorge is closest, about four feet away. Chano stands at the desk, his back turned. Aldo is on the other side of it, near the exit.

When Jorge turns toward him, Travis raises the .380 and shoots him through the right eye.

The noise is a sharp crack, loud in the confines of the office. Aldo pulls up the tail of his jersey, tugs at the gun in his waistband. Travis drops him with a forehead shot.

Chano reaches toward the drawer. Travis locks an arm around his throat, drags him back, the chair falling over. He aims the Ruger at the office door, waits. Pounding feet on the steps. Travis times it, fires twice through the shade, blowing out the glass. He hears the dreadlocked man fall. The shade flaps and rolls upward.

"Don't do this, homes," Chano says. "We can talk about it, work this out."

"You got more people outside?"

Chano doesn't answer. Travis touches the hot muzzle to his cheekbone. He flinches, tries to twist away. Travis tightens his grip. "Anyone outside?"

"No." Angry now. "Why you do this?"

"Simpler this way," Travis says, spins him around and shoots him in the face.

Gunsmoke hangs in the air. He goes to the door, stands to the side as he opens it. The dreadlocked man is facedown on the steps. Travis fires once into the back of his head.

He waits, listens for the front and side doors. The jet noise has faded. All he can hear is the wind, the slow ticking of the clock on the office wall.

It takes him a few minutes to find all the shell casings. One's on the desktop, near the photo. Drops of blood are spattered on the glass.

He cinches the money belt around his waist again, pulls on his jacket, uses a sleeve to smudge the office doorknob. He hasn't touched anything else.

At the side exit, he takes a rag from a workbench, uses it to undo the locks, then pushes the door open, the gun already up. Cold wind blows in. There's no one in the alley.

The gun at his side, he walks down to the empty street. It's clear. He gets out his burner cell, calls Cosmo. "I'm turning onto Mulberry. Pick me up."

"How'd it go?"

Travis ends the call. Another plane crosses low overhead.

He pockets the gun, draws in the night air, counts six slow breaths. At the next corner, he stands under a streetlight, raises his right hand in front of his face, fingers spread. He holds it there until it's perfectly still.

EIGHT

———

JOETTE WAKES WITH a feeling of dread. It's formless, seems to fill her, command her. The same thought again: *Get it out of here.*

By eight-thirty she's in the car, a zippered shoulder bag full of money on the passenger seat. She left behind $10,000 in hundreds in the suitcase. For emergencies, she told herself. Later, she'll find a better place to hide it. She'd burned the two charred bills in the kitchen sink the night before, washed the black ashes down the drain.

The first bank is a PNC in Toms River, about thirty miles south. She rents a safe-deposit box, fills it with $63,500 in strapped bills. Another $9,000 goes into a checking account. She knows a cash deposit of $10,000 or more would be reported to the IRS and red-flagged by Homeland Security.

Three more banks, and the bag is empty. She feels better

now, safer. She's running late, but instead of heading to the motel, she drives east on Route 33 to the shore. She parks in Ocean Grove, in one of the diagonal spots along the boardwalk. All the others are empty.

Wind moves the dune grass. She walks out onto the empty fishing pier, hands in her vest pockets against the cold. Two surfers in black wet suits are paddling out past the breakers. On the horizon, a container ship makes its way north to New York Harbor.

Waves crash against the pilings below. She hasn't been here in years, but the memories come back sharp and clear. Walking the boardwalk with Troy, hand in hand. Lying on the beach in summer, his head in her lap, watching banner planes drone by overhead. The two of them swimming out as far as they could, until the lifeguard's whistle called them back.

Before Troy, none of her relationships had lasted long, mostly through her own fault. With Troy, everything was different. *She* was different. The way he made her feel, the intensity of it, she'd never experienced before.

She hadn't considered marriage before, but with Troy it seemed inevitable. From the day they met, she knew things had changed forever. He saved her life, but she couldn't save his.

The surfers climb onto their boards, catching waves as they roll toward the beach. She closes her eyes, feels the wind, imagines Troy standing next to her.

Baby, she thinks. *You won't believe what I've done.*

———————

Lunch is a Chinese food delivery, ordered off one of the menus in the top drawer of the desk. She eats pork fried rice out of its container with a plastic fork, watching a rerun of *Who Wants to Be a Millionaire?*

The chimes ring. Cara comes in, carefully closes the door behind her. She climbs up on a chair beside the brochure rack. Her feet don't reach the floor.

"Hey, kiddo," Joette says. "What's doing?"

Cara shrugs, pushes a lock of pale blond hair from her eyes, looks up at the TV. "Can I turn on Cartoon Network?"

"Where's your mom?"

"Sleeping."

Joette looks up at the clock. It's just past noon.

"Here. Don't drop it." She lobs the remote into Cara's lap. Cara turns it around, starts to surf through channels.

"What did you do all morning?" Joette says.

"I was watching TV, but my mom said she needed to sleep and made me turn it off. So I finished reading my book instead."

"When do you go back to school?"

"Next week."

"How do you like sixth grade?"

"It's *boring*. I'd rather read my books."

The food is heavy in Joette's stomach, and she can feel a headache coming on. The container's still half full when she folds the top shut, drops it in the wastebasket behind the desk. She keeps the napkins and fortune cookie.

"You eat breakfast today?" she says.

"Cheerios. I got them myself."

Joette goes into the back room, gets a box of Snickers down from the supply shelf. She opens it with a box cutter and takes a bar from one of the forty-eight-count retail cartons.

"Heads up," she says as she comes back out. She holds up the bar, feints a throw. Cara raises her hands to catch it, frowns.

"What do you say?"

"Please."

Joette tosses her the bar. "And?"

"Thank you."

"You're welcome. Don't get chocolate on the remote."

Cara pulls the Snickers wrapper open, neatly peels back the paper. Joette doesn't know the cartoon, but Cara is watching it intently, not smiling, nibbling at the candy bar. Joette feels something pull inside her.

She unwraps the fortune cookie, snaps it in two and pulls out the strip of paper. It reads *Don't be afraid to take that big step.*

"There's your boyfriend," Cara says.

A cruiser is turning into the lot, Noah at the wheel, talking on a cell phone.

"Don't be a smart-ass," Joette says.

"He is, isn't he?"

"No, he's not."

"Then how do you know him?"

"We went to high school together, that's all."

Noah gets out, puts the phone away. The chimes sound as he comes in. "Hey, Jo. Hi, Carrie."

"Cara."

"What?"

"My name's Cara. Not Carrie."

"Sorry, Cara. My mistake." To Joette, he says, "Was driving by, thought I'd drop in for a minute, see how you were making out."

"With what?"

"Dealing with things." He looks at Cara, then back at Joette. "From the other day."

"I know about the car accident," Cara says, still looking at the TV. "My mom told me."

"I'm okay," Joette says.

"How's the arm?"

"Itches."

"You want to make sure it doesn't get infected. Let me take you to the walk-in."

"I'm fine. They find out anything more about the driver? There wasn't much in the paper."

"Troopers are handling it. State road, so it's their jurisdiction. They're not always quick to share information with the locals."

"He have family around here?"

"Troopers are on it, Jo. I'm sure they notified whoever they had to."

"And that's it?"

"What else did you expect?"

"To find out more, I guess. Where he was coming from, where he was headed, what he did for a living. Anything."

"You know as much as I do. It's not our case."

"Will the troopers come back? Will they want to talk to me again?"

"No, why would they? They took your statement, that's all they needed. Pretty clear what happened."

She feels herself relax. "I was just curious. Thanks for checking up on me."

"You change your mind about the clinic, I'll take you there."

He tousles Cara's hair as he leaves. They watch him drive off, the cell phone to his ear again.

"Why aren't you married?" Cara says. She's finished the Snickers bar.

"You don't quit, do you?" Joette hands her the napkins. "Here, Chocolate Face."

"My mom says you were."

"I was, once. Not anymore."

"Neither is my mom. She used to be, though, to my dad. His name's Rory. He lives in Ohio. He moved there after I was born."

"Have you ever met him?"

She shakes her head, wipes her face and folds the wrapper inside one of the napkins. "My mom doesn't like it when I ask about him. She says it makes her sad."

"When you're an adult, things don't always work out the way you want them to," Joette says. "That can be hard to get over sometimes."

"Maybe I'll meet him someday."

"Maybe you will."

"How far away is Ohio?"

"Not that far."

"When were you married?"

"Give it a break, kiddo."

"Was it a long time ago?"

"Sometimes it feels that way," Joette says.

"Did you have kids?"

"No, we didn't."

"Where is he now?"

"He got sick."

"Did he die?"

"Yes."

"I'm sorry."

Something tugs inside her again, sharper this time.

"I am too," she says.

NINE

WISH YOU'D TOLD me what you were going to do," Cosmo says.

They're in the cluttered back office of Cosmo's laundromat, on a side street in Red Bank. He's nervous behind the desk, chair rolled back, elbows on his knees. Under his suit jacket is a Hawaiian shirt, red flowers blooming on a black background.

"Wouldn't have made any difference," Travis says. "Way I saw it, there wasn't a choice."

He looks up at the monitor on the wall. It shows four views of the laundromat, rows of washers and dryers. All the customers are women, most of them Hispanic. Two small children are chasing each other around the machines. The manager, a young Salvadoran woman with long black hair, sits at the counter behind bulletproof glass, looking at her phone.

Travis nods at the screen. "I always wondered. Are you nailing her?"

"Esme? She works for me."

"Is that a yes?"

"Tell me about Chano. You believed him, about the money?"

"Far as it goes."

"So they didn't take it?"

"If they had, I don't think he would have met with me. Or he would have had his guys pop me as soon as I walked in the door. But he didn't. He was willing to talk. I showed him the ten grand. He knew there was more coming."

"Then why kill him?"

"He didn't trust us anymore. And I didn't trust him. Sooner or later he would have made his move. Couldn't take that chance."

"It's a lost cause either way, isn't it?" Cosmo says. "Maybe Tommy stashed the money on his way back, didn't want it with him when he got to a hospital. He could've thrown it in the woods somewhere, was going to come back and get it. It might be anyplace. Could be somebody already found it. Whatever, it's gone."

"What I'm wondering is what his plan was. If he thought he was gonna walk out of there with both the money and the product, he had to have a way to get clear fast. He wasn't going to hang around, wait for someone to come looking for him."

"Whatever plan he had, it didn't do him much good."

"How are you on a new connect?"

"Working on it. Nothing yet. We're just about out of product, too, and I've got buyers waiting."

"The Ds can't be the only ones bringing in fent."

"Only ones in that quantity and quality right now," Cosmo

says. "Anyway, even if I do find someone, we need front cash. And we're short on that at the moment, if you hadn't noticed. Every time we solve one problem, there's another right behind it."

"Comes with the territory. You're not back at Rutgers selling pot to frat boys."

"Don't knock it. I made a lot of money back then, moved a shit-ton of weed. That business degree paid for itself. Then, when X and Molly came in, forget it. Twenty-eight years old, I had so much cash coming in I didn't know what to do with it. That's how I financed this place."

"And every scumbag in Jersey wanted a piece of your action. Until you met me."

"I never said otherwise, T. I owe you."

"I handled things then, I'll handle them now."

"Nothing gets to you, does it?" Cosmo says. "You take everything in stride. This was supposed to be a straight-up money deal. Invest, recoup, make a profit. Now where are we?"

"What's done is done."

"And when Chano's people figure out what happened, and come after us?"

"Let them," Travis says.

––––––––––

He watches the Escalade pull off the Parkway into the rest area. It drives past empty spots, parks near his truck. The man who gets out is wearing a suit and overcoat, but his shaved head, thick neck and Oakley sunglasses scream cop.

"Let's make this fast," he says when he gets in the truck. "I'm on duty soon."

"What do you have for me?"

"Accident report." He takes folded papers from an inside pocket, hands them over.

New Jersey State Police letterhead. Two typed sheets of notes, a third page with a diagram of the accident, then printouts of color photos—a burned-out car from different angles, close-ups of skid marks on the road. The car is black and gutted, but he recognizes Tommy's BMW.

The trooper pushes his sunglasses up on his scalp. "Nice truck. Looks new. What's it go for stock, about thirty-five?"

Travis looks through the pages. "There's not much here."

"It's what Cosmo asked for."

"Is this public record?"

"It will be when the investigation's finished."

"So why am I paying you?"

"Don't fuck with me, brother. I owe Cosmo a favor. Only reason I'm here."

"Glove compartment."

The trooper opens it, takes out the white envelope, checks the money inside. Five hundreds.

"Tell me about this woman," Travis says. "The witness."

"Harper? Nothing to tell. She works at that motel, saw the whole thing." He puts the envelope in a coat pocket, shuts the glove box.

"You talk to her?"

"No. The troopers who responded did. Her statement's in there."

"So you weren't at the scene."

"Didn't have to be. No mystery there. Driver was bleeding out from an abdominal GSW, lost control, hit that abutment doing forty, forty-five. They did a crash reconstruction afterward."

"He was dead when the EMTs arrived?"

"That's what it says. They pronounced him there."

"Anything else inside the car?"

"Like what?"

"Anything unusual."

"You see anything in the report?"

"I'm asking if there's anything wasn't in the report."

"Why are you so interested in an MVA?"

Travis doesn't answer, looks at the photos again.

"We done here?" the trooper says.

Travis folds the pages, tucks them between the seat and console. "Yeah, we're done."

"Tell Cosmo we're square." He gets out. Travis watches him walk back to the Escalade.

Everybody's got their hand out, he thinks. Cops, too. Risk everything—their careers, their freedom—for some extra cash, and the feeling they're getting over on the world.

He waits until the Escalade is gone, then pulls the truck out onto the Parkway and heads north.

In Jersey City, he finds the body shop from memory. It's in a warehouse area a few blocks from the new town houses and high-rises on the waterfront. He can see the Statue of Liberty in the distance.

The shop's closed, metal gates pulled over the windows. He drives by slow. They'll have cleaned up in there. No need to go inside.

He heads south again, tracing the route Tommy would have taken back through Monmouth County. Dark now. Leaving the Parkway, he turns south onto Route 34, passes strip malls and car dealerships, then business parks, sand and gravel companies. Woods spring up on both sides of the highway. Signs advertise land for lease and sale.

He can see the motel now, ahead on the left. An ancient neon sign lights up the lot. Just past it is the bridge.

He pulls onto the shoulder, looks across at the motel. A single car is parked outside the attached A-frame office. Through the front window, he can see a woman at the counter.

No reason to wait. He swings the truck back onto the road, cuts across both lanes and pulls into the lot.

TEN

———

JOETTE WATCHES THE big black Chevy truck pull in, park beside her Subaru. She takes the remote from the counter, mutes Oprah.

The driver takes his time getting out. He's in his thirties, longish dark hair, wearing jeans and boots, a brown work jacket over a black T-shirt.

The chimes sound.

"Can I help you?" she says.

"Hope so." He gives her a crooked smile. He's attractive in a rough way, unshaven. His eyes look blue at first, but as he comes up to the counter she sees they're pale gray.

"I'm working a construction job down here for a few weeks. I'm looking for a place to stay that's close by."

"Just you?"

"Just me. I've been commuting from up in Paterson."

"That's a drive."

"Feels even longer when you have a ten-hour day, starts at seven in the morning. And the Turnpike traffic on top of that. Decided it would be easier to get a place around here for the duration. I drove by, saw the lot, figured you had some rooms available." The smile again.

"It's seventy-five a night," she says. "Ninety-five on Friday and Saturday. The weekly rate's five hundred. Monthly's fifteen."

"A little steep for this time of year, isn't it? Doesn't look like you're doing much business."

"I don't set the prices. All the rooms are efficiencies. Air conditioning, kitchenette with refrigerator and microwave."

"I didn't see a pool."

"We don't have one. But there's a picnic area out back, with a propane grill guests can use. Vending machines on the side."

He looks at the curtained doorway. "Is it just you here?"

She puts the clipboard with the registration forms on the counter, sets a ball-point pen atop it. "Why don't you go ahead and fill that out."

He looks at the clipboard but doesn't pick it up. "Old-school. No computer. This place is classic."

"I'll need a driver's license and credit card."

"Just looking, remember?"

He scratches his flat stomach through the T-shirt. There's a spiderweb tattoo on the back of his right hand. His wrists are thick.

"Where's the job?" she says.

"On Route Thirty-Three, where the old drive-in used to be?"

She knows the site. Undeveloped for years, now just weeds

coming up through blacktop, rows of decapitated speaker poles. She saw construction vehicles there last week, has been caught in slow traffic passing the site, one lane blocked off with cones.

"What are they building?"

"Condos. What else."

"What do you do?"

"Whatever they need. Run equipment mostly. Bulldozers, front-end loaders. I do it all."

"Must pay well."

"The truck? Hell, the bank owns most of that."

"What outfit you work for?"

"Ankrum Brothers." She knows the name, has seen their equipment around.

Maybe you're just paranoid, she thinks. *Your nerves are shot.*

"Anything else you want to know?" he says.

"I have to ask. We don't get many walk-ins this time of year. And the owner doesn't like to rent to transients."

"I don't blame him. You must see a lot of crazy stuff here."

"Not really. Usually it's pretty quiet."

"Heard you had some excitement the other day, though."

"Excitement?"

"An accident out front. Car caught fire, but someone pulled the driver out. Was that you?"

"Where did you hear that?" Watching his face.

"Local news station, 101.5. All the driving I do, I listen to the radio a lot. I heard about the accident, remembered the name—Castaways. It hit me as I pulled in that this was the place."

"I didn't know the name was in the news stories."

"It was, in the one I heard, at least. Didn't realize it was a secret."

"No secret. Just a surprise to hear we were mentioned."

He massages his knuckles. "You see it happen? The actual crash?"

She looks past him to the highway, aware of how alone she is here. "I did."

"Guy must have been drunk or high or something, smash up a car like that."

"I wouldn't know."

"Pretty bad shape when you got to him, I imagine. Was he alive?"

A dark Denali with smoked windows pulls in, hip-hop music thumping inside. She feels a sudden wave of relief. It parks outside room four, and Brianna and Cara get out. At the room, Brianna turns and waves to the driver. He gives a quick double tap on the horn, then swings around and drives off, the music fading.

"So this place isn't empty after all," the man says.

"I've got some things to tend to. I don't mean to be rude, but if you're not interested in a room..."

"Sorry. Didn't mean to take up your time."

"Fill out that form, and it'll be ready to go if you decide to come back."

"I'm good for now, thanks."

When he's at the door, she says, "I didn't get your name."

"Didn't give it." He grins again. "See you again soon, maybe."

As he gets in the truck, she picks up the pen, drops it, retrieves it just as he pulls onto the highway. She writes the license number in the margin of the registration form. Her hand is shaking.

———

Driving back to Keansburg, Travis plays it through in his mind again. He watched the woman's eyes, trying to read her reaction, wondering if she'd bought his story. He drove by that construction site on Route Thirty-Three a few days ago, saw the Ankrum Brothers name on equipment there.

It rattled her when he said he'd heard the name of the motel on the radio, a straight-up lie. He sensed the wariness then, her drawing back.

In his apartment above the hardware store, he gets a Heineken from the refrigerator, drinks it at the breakfast counter, reads the state police report again. There's not much to her statement. She described the accident, pulling Tommy from the car. No way to know how long he lived, if he said anything to her before he died. When she got him out of the car, he might already have been unconscious, either from blood loss or the accident. He went up there looking to make the biggest score of his life, ended up gutshot and dying by the side of the road.

But there was something about her, the way she played it close with him. It might just be nerves from the accident, or something she wasn't telling him, hadn't told the state police.

He doesn't like it. He needs order, to know where things stand. The woman bothers him.

Who are you, Joette Harper? he thinks. *And what are you hiding?*

ELEVEN

F ORGET IT, JO," Noah says. "No way."

She's standing at the office window, looking out at the highway, cell phone to her ear. "Why not? You do it all the time. When you pull someone over, you run their plates, don't you? See if they have any warrants or priors?"

"Yeah, when I pull somebody over. Then it's procedure. But just to check up on someone, get their personal info? That has to go through a supervisor, and you need a good reason for asking. This isn't. And I'm not sure what the issue here is. You didn't rent him a room."

"He didn't want one."

"Well, if he comes back and he does, don't give him one. Make up some excuse. What was it about him got under your skin, anyway?"

"Just a feeling. I thought you could run the plate, get

his name. Maybe he has a criminal record, something that would flag him in your computer system. That's not much to ask, is it?"

"If that's all you have to go on, yeah, it is. And an invasion of privacy at that. You know what I think?"

"What?"

"You're still a little shook up from the other day. Sounds to me like you're getting worked up over nothing."

"Like a woman?"

"I didn't say that."

"But it's what you meant."

"Listen, Jo. Odds are you'll never see him again. If you do, and he gives you a hard time about anything, call me. If you're scared or think you're in danger, call 911."

"Jesus, this isn't much help."

"As much as I can do for you at this point. Guy's done nothing wrong, or even suspicious, from what you say. I get the vibe thing, but I think you might be a little hyper sensitive right now."

Her thumb hovers over the End key. "I shouldn't have called."

"You want, I'll go over to that jobsite, talk to him. Not sure what it'll accomplish, but if it'll make you feel better…"

"No. Don't do that. Forget about it."

"You sure you're okay?"

You have no idea.

"Maybe you're right. Delayed reaction from the accident."

"Happens that way. Things catch up with you. I'm on until midnight, but I can swing by the trailer afterward if you want, pick you up. We can get a late drink somewhere."

"I appreciate the offer, but I don't think I'm up for it tonight. Some other time."

"Might be good, unwind a little. You change your mind, let me know."

"I will," she says.

———————

A sharp tap on the glass. Joette jumps. She's been nodding at the desk, drowsy from the warmth of the heater, the TV on low. Brianna is shivering outside the door, wearing a thin leather jacket, yoga pants and a Metallica T-shirt.

Joette buzzes her in, looks at the clock. Nine-thirty already.

"Cold out there," Brianna says.

"Don't you have a winter coat?"

"It's on my list. The one that keeps getting longer."

Joette waits, knows what's coming.

"I know I'm late," Brianna says. "And I know I said it wouldn't happen again. It'll just be a few more days, though. Malcolm's promised me shifts all weekend. I can have the whole month's rent for you on Monday, or bring some by on Saturday, whatever I have, cash. Hand it right over to you."

"Singh hasn't asked me yet. But he will. Have you thought about what you'll do this summer?"

"K-Rock says he'll help us find a place. Hopefully soon."

"K-Rock?"

"Keith. Everybody calls him K-Rock. When he dropped us off, I wanted him to come in, say hello. Told him how good you've been to me and Cara. He was in a hurry, though, said next time. He's a decent guy, really."

"What's he do?"

"He's at Home Depot, you know the one on Sixty-Six? His boss likes him. They don't care that he did a little time.

A lot of places do. It's not fair. Someone gets out, wants to make a new start, they should get the chance."

"He have kids?"

"A boy, Cody. Younger than Cara, but they get along. He lives with Keith's mom. We want to find a place we can all be together."

Joette thinks about the ten thousand in the trailer, what it would mean to Brianna, what it could do for Cara.

"What about Cody's mom?" Joette says. "She in the picture?"

"Not anymore. Good thing, too. She wasn't much of a mother."

Joette's not sure what to say but has to say something, what she's been holding back.

"I hope it works out for all of you. I worry about you two, especially Cara. Being around this place all the time, it's not good. Not healthy."

Brianna looks away. When she turns back, her eyes are wet. "You think I don't know that?"

Joette feels bad, like she's overstepped. She wants to apologize, then stops herself.

"Give me what you can Saturday, even if it's a little. I'll cover for you on the rest until you can come up with it. I won't tell Singh."

"I'll get it all to you as soon as I can. Promise."

After Brianna leaves, Joette feels a vague depression settling over her. She shuts off the TV, watches headlights pass on the highway. Wishes she were anywhere but here.

———————

The gas station is a quarter mile south of the motel, on the opposite side of the highway. It's closed for the night. Parked alongside the building, Travis has a clear view of the motel lot, the Subaru. He's been here an hour already, watched the traffic thin.

At 10:15, a station wagon passes him, the muffler loud, turns into the motel. A man lumbers inside the office. After a few minutes, the Harper woman comes out, gets into the Subaru. She turns north out of the lot, away from him.

He starts the engine and pulls onto the highway after her, headlights off. The truck rattles across the creek bridge.

She's easy to follow. The Subaru's right taillight lens is cracked, white light showing through. After a mile, he turns on his lights, but hangs back. He's not worried about her getting too far ahead. The truck can close the distance in seconds.

She gets on Route 18, heading east. Few cars here, so he has to stay farther back. But when she exits in Eatontown, the highway's busy with traffic coming off the Parkway. This stretch of road is brightly lit, lined with hotels, commuter lots and chain restaurants.

He follows her onto Route 35 South, has to slow when her brake lights go on. She pulls into a strip mall lot. A handful of cars are parked outside a storefront with a sign that reads VICTORY BAR & LIQUORS. The rest of the lot is empty. There's a nail salon on one side of the bar, a deli on the other, both dark.

He takes the jug handle a quarter mile ahead, doubles back and pulls into the lot. He parks at the far end, dims his lights. He turns off the engine and waits.

———

Doreen's working the back bar, as Joette hoped she would be. She draws a pint of Blue Moon, sets it on a bar coaster as Joette sits down.

"Hey, doll," Doreen says. "Haven't seen you in a while."

She's somewhere north of fifty, but Joette doesn't know how much. She's deeply tanned all year, with a swimmer's body and toned arms. Her sleeveless blue work shirt is un-buttoned far enough to show the tattoo on her collarbone—STAY STRONG in dark floral script.

Joette puts a twenty on the bar. "What's your secret?"

"For what?"

"Never aging."

"I wish."

Joette got a gym membership not long after Troy died, hoping regular exercise would help her start to feel better. But she rarely made it there, despite what she was paying, and eventually let the membership lapse. Not going had just become something else to feel bad about.

She takes a pull from the beer, scans the ten or so faces at the U-shaped bar. Only regulars and serious drinkers here. No twentysomethings or slumming hipsters. A place she can come alone and be left alone. She feels guilty for turning Noah down but needed time to think. And she wasn't sure if, after a few drinks, she could trust herself not to tell him more.

"You want singles for the jukebox?" Doreen says.

"Please."

She feeds dollar bills into the machine, pushes buttons, choosing the same R&B songs she always does. B. B. King's "The Thrill Is Gone" kicks in as she goes back to her seat. "How's Vic?"

"Stress test last week," Doreen says. "No more blockages, thankfully. They gave him some new meds to keep his blood pressure and cholesterol under control, but I have to stay on him to take them. You'd think a heart attack at fifty-five would throw a scare into someone, make him change his ways. Not my guy."

"He still smoking?"

"Says he's not, but I smell it on him sometimes. I think he sneaks them when I'm not around. It drives me crazy. I was a wreck when he was in the hospital that last time. That night in the ER, the chest pains he was having, I thought I was going to lose him."

She opens Bud Lites for a pair of Central American workers on the other side of the bar, takes their empties. They're silently watching a soccer match on the overhead TV.

Joette sips beer, trying to lose the sense of unease she's felt since seeing the man in the Chevy truck. She remembers the spiderweb tattoo, the thick wrists. She wonders if he'll come back.

"Slow tonight," she says to Doreen. It's late, but she doesn't want to go home.

"Way it's been lately."

"Do a shot with me."

"Cuervo?"

"All day."

Doreen sets out shot glasses, takes a bottle from the speed rack. Etta James on the jukebox now, "At Last."

They tap glasses. Joette sips the tequila. It's smooth and warm going down. It seems to steady her. She tries to relax.

Doreen refills their glasses.

"Hard-core," Joette says.

"Life's short."

"We don't get smarter, though, do we? Just older."

"Truth."

They drink. Joette chases the shot with a swallow of beer. *Careful. Last thing you need is a DWI on the way home.*

"You look like you've got something on your mind," Doreen says. "Things getting to you?"

"Just thinking."

"About?"

"How so many times in my life, I thought I had it all figured out. Knew who I was, where I was going. And it always turned out I didn't know anything at all."

"You have to cut yourself some slack. We've all made bad decisions."

"Believe me, I have made some *very* bad decisions."

"So have I," Doreen says. "But you know the Serenity Prayer, right? 'Lord, grant me the serenity' and all that?"

"Sure."

"Well, there's a shorter version."

"Is there?"

"There is. And all it says is 'Fuck it.'"

———

He watches her come out of the bar, waits for the Subaru to pull back onto the highway, then follows her again. Only a short distance this time, a half mile at most. She signals and makes a right at a sign that reads BRIGHT PINES VILLAGE.

He drives past. Ahead on the right is a vacant restaurant, brown paper on the inside windows, a RETAIL SPACE AVAILABLE sign. He pulls in, reverses into the shadows alongside the building, shuts down the engine.

He waits there in darkness, watching cars go by, giving her time. After a half hour, he gets out, cuts through parking lots and stands of pines, estimating distances, following the highway but staying back from the shoulder.

Past the last screen of trees is the chain-link fence that borders the trailer park's main street. It's laid out in a simple grid. The main road is one-way. It runs through the park to the far end, then curves around and heads back to the highway exit. Shorter secondary streets run north and south.

He grips the metal diamonds of the fence, gets the toes of his boots in, pulls himself up. Swinging his hips over the top bar, he drops down easily on the other side.

Most of the trailers are dark. Staying close to the fence, he moves deeper into the park. Fighting cats screech somewhere nearby.

Her trailer is easy to find, the Subaru parked in the carport alongside it. He watches from across the road. Lights are on inside the trailer, the blinds and curtains drawn. A silhouette moves past a window. No voices inside. She's alone.

———————

Joette gets a Blue Moon from the refrigerator, brings it into the bedroom. She opens the bottom drawer of the dresser, takes out the framed photo. It's an eight-by-ten blowup from a cell phone shot. She and Troy in a two-person kayak on the Delaware, six months before his diagnosis. Her face is in the foreground as she holds the phone at arm's length. Both of them smiling and sunburned, wearing orange life vests and blue baseball caps. Neither of them with any idea what lay ahead.

Was I ever that young? Was I ever that happy?

The photo used to hang on the bedroom wall, but there came a time when it was too painful to look at. It only reminded her of the distance between what her life had been and what it was now.

Those last three months, when he was in and out of the hospital, were the worst of it. A roller coaster of hope and fear that left her exhausted and numb. Months behind on mortgage payments and medical bills, she finally gave up the house, let them foreclose. It felt as if she were watching it all from a distance, everything unraveling, unable to stop it. After a while, she quit trying. Nothing seemed to matter anymore.

The payout on his life insurance bought the trailer. She fended off the endless bills as best she could. For a while, she considered leaving New Jersey, starting fresh somewhere else. Then came her mother's stroke, and again everything changed, her future decided for her. There was no going anywhere then.

She brings the photo into the living room, sets it on the end table beside the couch. It feels right to have it out again now, to have him there with her.

Travis watches the trailer for a long time, picturing her in there alone. When the last light goes out, he turns and walks back to his truck.

TWELVE

SHE DREAMS ABOUT Troy, wakes feeling anxious and unsettled. She pushes off the comforter, tries to remember the details of the dream, but they're gone.

It's overhot in the trailer, the air dry. Nine a.m. She needs to get moving but doesn't want to get out of bed.

What you get for going to sleep half drunk.

Sunlight pours through the bedroom window. She flashes back to a summer morning at their house in Point Pleasant, a month or so after they were married. Troy asleep beside her, snoring softly. She was propped up on an elbow, watching him, the fall of light across his face and hair, remembers thinking, *How did I get so lucky?*

Grief is a sea, a counselor told her, at one of the group meetings she went to just after his death. Sometimes it's flat and calm. Other days, a sudden wave can drag you under without warning.

So many times she thought she was on her way to feeling better, only to have something bring her crashing down again. The triggers were always there, waiting. A song, a photo, a phrase he used. She had to learn to resist the impulse to cling to things that reminded her of him. She knows why she did it. Feeling bad was better than not feeling anything at all.

She showers, dresses. No time for breakfast. She'll have to wait to eat, order takeout again.

When she pulls into the motel lot, the black Chevy pickup is parked outside the office. The man from yesterday is sitting on a wrought-iron chair outside room four, working on Cara's pink bicycle with a wrench, while Cara and Brianna watch. Brianna holds the bike steady for him, talking away, making eye contact whenever he looks up. He lifts his chin at Joette when she gets out of the car.

In the office, Baxter is watching *Family Feud*. "You're late. Again."

"How long has he been here?" she says.

"Who?"

"That man outside, with Cara and Bree."

"Not long. He was looking for you."

"Why?"

"I don't know. I told him you were supposed to be here at ten. It's ten-twenty." He takes his jacket from the wall peg.

"He asked for me by name?" she says. "What else did he say?"

"Only that he wanted to talk to you."

"Stranger comes in off the street, asks about me, you tell him, 'Stick around, she'll be here soon'?"

"How was I supposed to know he was a stranger? He acted like he knew you."

"Never mind." She raises the hinged panel, moves behind the counter. "Anything happen overnight?"

"If it did, I didn't hear about it."

He goes out and starts his station wagon. It coughs gray smoke as he drives away. She finds the remote, shuts off the TV.

The man's at the door. He wipes his hands on a rag before opening it. He's clean-shaven today.

"Morning," he says. "Hoped I'd catch you."

"Why's that?"

"I was a little rude yesterday. Wanted to apologize."

"Nothing to apologize for."

"I met your other tenants. Brianna—that her name?—and Cara. We got to talking. They told me about the bike, said she hadn't been able to ride it for a while. I said bring it out, I'll take a look."

"That was kind of you."

"Chain was slipping. No big deal. Had some tools in the truck. That Brianna likes to talk."

"She does."

"Cara's a smart kid. Quiet, though. You were the same way at her age, I bet."

She closes the panel, feeling the first edge of fear. "What can I do for you?"

"Still trying to decide on a place to stay. Narrowing it down. Had another question, though. An important one."

"What's that?"

"If I stay here, let's say two or three weeks, is there a problem paying cash? In advance, of course."

"You could have asked Baxter that."

"The night man? Nice-enough guy, but he didn't seem

too sharp, to be honest. Wasn't sure I could trust his answer."

"We take cash but still need a credit card for a deposit."

"That's an issue, why I ask. Dumped all my cards, don't use them anymore. Helps me keep my finances manageable."

"Three weeks' rent is a lot of cash to be carrying around."

"I think you're onto me."

She watches his eyes. "How's that?"

"I'm off the books when I work for the brothers. I should have told you that. Maybe you called over there, asked about me."

"I didn't."

"Easier for them to pay me cash, under the table, than deal with Uncle Sam. Better for me, too. No taxes. Guess I shouldn't be telling you all this."

"None of my business. Leave your name and cell number. I'll talk to the owner, see if he'll give you a better rate for cash. Maybe he'll let you slide on the deposit."

"I don't want to put you to any trouble."

"No trouble."

"I've still got a couple other places to visit. Thanks for your time, though. One other thing."

"What?"

"I don't really know anybody down this way, and there isn't much to do around here this time of year. Would you like to get a drink some night, when you're off? I'd welcome the company."

"I don't think that's a good idea. We're not supposed to fraternize with guests."

Fraternize? Where did that come from?

"I'm not a guest yet, though, am I? Sorry if I'm out of line. Didn't see a ring, so I assumed you were single. Can't blame me for asking, can you?"

She doesn't respond. Waits him out.

"Anyway," he says. "It was good talking to you again."

"You never told me your name."

At the door, he turns, grins. "Travis."

"Travis what?"

"Just Travis. See you around, Joette."

———————

He makes his way back to the laundromat. Cosmo buzzes him into the office.

"I have a connect," Cosmo says. "But we're still shy."

Travis takes the seat across from his desk. "Who is it?"

"Some bikers out of Philly. Wouldn't normally deal with them—too unpredictable. But you're right, we lose our regulars, our market share'll be fucked for good. We do a deal with these guys, turn it over quick, it keeps us going. Hopefully it's a one-off, we won't need to do it again."

A headache is blooming in Travis's left temple. He thinks about Joette Harper at the motel that morning, alone in her trailer the night before. He hasn't told Cosmo about finding her.

"What are they asking?"

"Seventy a key."

"Hell with that."

"It cuts into our profit margin," Cosmo says. "But it'll keep the tap flowing while I find someone farther up the food chain with a better price."

"How shy are we on the seventy?"

"Twenty K left in the pool money, so we're fifty short. And we could have a time issue here."

"Why?"

"They don't know us. If we come up with the seventy quick, we're for real. If we can't, then we're not."

"What do we have left in product?"

"A few grams, already cut, that's it. Our doc from Manahawkin called today, wants ten as soon as we can get it, has the cash ready. I tried to convince him to front us, but he wouldn't do it."

"He doesn't trust us after all this time? Fuck him."

"Fent's like everything else that came before it," Cosmo says. "Everybody wants in before the bubble bursts. And it will, just like crack did. In the meantime, he's trying to put as much money in his pockets as he can. Just like everybody."

"Seventy K."

"Told them I'd have an answer by the end of the week. If it's yes, we gotta show money right away. Seller's market right now. That worked for us in the past. Now it's working against us."

Travis rubs the back of his neck, the tight muscles there.

"What are you thinking?" Cosmo says.

"I'm thinking sometimes it feels like this shit is hardly worth it."

"Look at it as a temporary setback," Cosmo says. "In the meantime, if we want to play, we gotta pay."

"Tell them we'll do the deal. Set it up for next week. We'll have the cash."

"What about the fifty?"

"Let me worry about that," Travis says.

THIRTEEN

MIDNIGHT. HE SITS in the Silverado, parked under a willow tree, lights off, watching the trap house up the block. Blinds are drawn in the front windows, showing slivers of light. The second floor is dark. There's an abandoned house on one side of the property, a cleared lot on the other. Woods across the street.

A light goes on over the side door. Truman comes out, limps down the street toward the truck. The door closes behind him, and the light goes out.

Travis powers down his window. "Did you cop?"

Truman nods. He's skinny and ragged, with a wispy beard, wearing a thin denim jacket. A meth-head when Travis first met him.

"How much?" Travis says.

"Three rocks."

"Let me see."

Truman holds up a plastic vial with a yellow cap. The clusters inside are more brown than white.

"That what Jimmy Mac's selling these days? How much he take you for?"

"Sixty. Twenty each. It's been dry around here."

"Fucking thief. How many people inside?"

"Three. Boy named T.C.'s got the door. Jimmy Mac and his old lady Sharon are on a couch in the living room."

"Anybody upstairs?"

"I don't think so."

"What's the deal with the front door?"

"Nailed shut, with one of those metal bars across it. Anyone wants to cop has to come around the side. I've been in there before. Nobody lives there, but the power's still on. They only use the house when the package comes in."

"Where's the rock?"

"It's all vialed up in another room. Kitchen, I think. T.C. takes the money."

"Back door?"

"Off the kitchen. Nailed up tight, same way."

"Who's carrying?"

"Jimmy's got that flash forty-five right there on the table, so everybody can see it. T.C.'s got something too, in his belt."

Travis pulls on a pair of leather gloves. He should be feeling the rush, getting ready. Instead he's tired. Pissed that he's back dealing with people like these.

"What's the backyard like?"

"Full of junk and trash. You can hear the rats."

A car comes down the street from the other direction, stops outside the house. The passenger gets out, a skinny black man in an army coat.

"See?" Truman says. "Like I told you. Busy all night."

The man knocks at the side door. The light goes on, and he talks to someone through the single pane of glass. The door opens, and he goes in.

"When did they get the package?" Travis says.

"This afternoon. They put the word out, so everyone knows it's there."

"What do they do with the cash?"

"I didn't stay to see. I just wanted to cop and get out fast."

Travis opens the center console, takes out the glassine bag with the single capsule inside, white powder in a clear gelcap. "Try a white man's drug for a change. Toss that other shit."

He hands Truman the bag. "It's been stepped on, but it started pure, so it's hotter than what you're used to. Cut it a couple more times and you're good for days. Hit it as is, and it'll kill you quick."

The skinny man comes out the side door again, gets back in the car. It U-turns, drives off. The light goes out.

"If you don't need me for anything else, I'm gonna book," Truman says.

"Go on."

When he doesn't move, Travis says, "What?"

"None of this is gonna come back on me, is it?"

"You tell anyone you were meeting me?"

"No."

"Then keep your mouth shut and you'll be fine."

Travis watches him in the side mirror as he limps away, trying to move fast, put distance between himself and whatever's going to happen. Just wants to get home and get high, Travis thinks. All he's been looking forward to. He'll ignore the warning, or forget it, and be dead by dawn.

He takes the Ruger from his jacket pocket, checks there's a round in the chamber.

Stop putting it off, he thinks. *Do what you came for.*

The dome light is off, so the cab stays dark when he gets out. The Ruger goes into his belt at the small of his back, the metal cold against his skin.

He knocks at the side door, waits, then knocks again, louder. The light goes on. A face at the glass. Black kid, late teens, early twenties. "What you want?"

"Here to see Jimmy. You T.C.?"

"Who are you?"

"Friend of Truman's."

"I don't know you."

Travis takes out a hundred-dollar bill, presses it to the glass. "Don't hang me up, brother. I'm hurting."

"Put that shit away."

Travis pockets the bill, flexes his right hand at his side to loosen it.

"What you looking for?" T.C. says.

"Same thing everybody is. I got the word."

T.C. works locks. The door opens a few inches. "How you know Truman?"

"From around the way. We go back."

"What's your name?"

"Benjamin. Don't leave me standing out here, bro. Make up your mind."

T.C. opens the door wider. Travis sees the butt of the gun in his belt. T.C. looks past Travis to the street. "Where's your car?"

"Down the block. I didn't think it was smart, pull up out front."

"Come inside. Wait right here. I mean *right* the fuck here."

He closes and locks the door behind him. "How much you want?"

"Much as that hundred will buy me."

On the right is a kitchen, lit by a shadeless table lamp on the floor. Down the hallway to the left is the doorway to the living room. Stairs to the right.

"This way," T.C. says.

When he turns, Travis takes out the Ruger, fires into the back of the head. Blood hits the wall. Travis steps over him as he falls, moves quickly into the living room. Jimmy Mac is coming up from the couch, fumbling with a chrome-plated automatic. Travis points the Ruger at him. "Set it down, Jimmy."

He's wearing black silk pants, a red shirt open to show gold chains against dark skin. His cornrows end in long beaded braids. He's heavier than the last time Travis saw him, his face rounder.

"Travis, what the fuck, man?"

"Put it on the floor and step away."

The woman on the couch has purple lipstick and eye shadow, long hair dyed black. There's a plastic bong on the low table in front of her, an open baggie of pot and a cheap lighter. The room smells of mildew and burning weed.

Jimmy holds up the .45 to show his finger's off the trigger. The gun has silver grips, an inlaid grinning skull on each side. He sets it on the hardwood floor. Travis kicks it across the room. "Sloppy setup, Jimmy. You used to know better."

"Who are you?" the woman says. "Do I know you?" Her eyes are bloodshot. She's too stoned to be scared.

Jimmy raises his hands. "Just chill, T. Let's talk this out."

The woman starts to stand, totters. "Who are you?" she says again.

"Sit down," Travis says.

"Sharon...," Jimmy says. But she's up, has her balance now, coming toward him. Travis switches the Ruger to his other hand, steps in and hits her in the cheekbone with his right fist, putting his shoulder into it. The impact twists her around. She's unconscious when she hits the floor.

"Shit, man," Jimmy says. "You didn't have to do that."

Travis takes zip ties from his jacket pocket, tosses them on the couch. "Do her hands in back. Feet, too. I don't want her coming at me again."

Jimmy takes the zip ties, kneels heavily beside her. He binds her wrists and ankles, then stands slowly, out of breath.

"Rock and green," Travis says. "All you got."

"Whatever you want, man. Just be cool."

"I am. Kitchen?"

"Yeah."

"Let's go."

Jimmy stops when he sees T.C., the pool of blood beneath his head. "That was cold."

"Go."

A rat runs along the kitchen baseboard, vanishes behind a toppled refrigerator. The single window is boarded over. As they move by the lamp, their shadows pass on the wall.

"Up there," Jimmy says.

"Get it."

Jimmy opens a cabinet, takes down a child's pale blue backpack.

"On the counter," Travis says.

Jimmy unzips it, dumps out the contents, tightly wound cylinders of money, each bound with a thick rubber band. Some of them show tens and fives. Dirty money. Street money.

"How much?" Travis says.

"Ten, last time we counted."

"That's it?"

"Rock doesn't move way it used to. People into other things."

"Where is it?"

"Underneath."

Travis gestures with the Ruger. Jimmy bends, takes out a small black trash bag from a cabinet beneath the sink. It's knotted at the top. He sets it on the counter, unties it and pulls the neck open so Travis can see the yellow-capped vials inside.

"All we got," Jimmy says.

Travis takes a folded nylon laundry bag from his back pocket, tosses it to him. "Put everything in there."

Jimmy fills the laundry bag with the vials, then the money, pulls the drawstring tight.

"Living room," Travis says. There might be more cash in the house, more rock. But he just wants to be gone from here, out of the smell, out of the memories.

On the floor, the woman moans. Her eyes are half closed, spittle on her lips.

"Why you do me like this?" Jimmy says. "We used to be tight."

Travis takes the bag from him. "I'm finished here, but I need you to get down there with her so I can do your hands too."

"No call for that. You walk out of here, I forget this ever happened, write this shit off. I'm just a middleman."

"I'm gonna need you to do it anyway. You'll work your way loose before long. Or someone will find you."

Jimmy kneels beside the woman, then lies down, crosses his wrists behind him. "For real, man. I won't say shit. Far as I'm concerned, I never even saw you."

"That's good."

"Like I said, I'm just a—"

"Middleman," Travis says, and fires twice.

An hour later, he's parked at a McDonald's off the highway a half hour east of Camden. The Ruger is pushed down between the seat and console.

A dark Navigator pulls in, does a circuit of the lot, then parks two spots away. Darnell Jackson gets out on the passenger side, walks over to the truck, gets in.

"Haven't heard from you in a minute," he says. "Surprised to get your call, middle of the night."

"Something came my way." Travis reaches behind the passenger seat, pulls out the old canvas knapsack he put the vials in, sets it at Darnell's feet.

"What's this?" Darnell says.

"Look and see."

Darnell opens the knapsack. "How much you got here?"

"Half a key, I'm guessing," Travis says. "Vialed and capped. Ready to move."

"Guessing?"

"Make an offer."

"You test it?"

"Wasn't time. But it's from a good source."

Darnell takes out a vial, holds it at an angle to catch the light from the pole lamp. "Looks rough."

"It's rock. It always looks rough."

He examines two more vials in the light. "Why you messing with this street shit?"

"You want it or not?"

Darnell puts the vials back in the bag. "Fifteen."

"Worth more than that. You know it."

"I'm betting you don't know your own self what you got here. And I'm wondering where it came from."

"Came from me. Isn't that enough?"

"Might be it belonged to someone holds a grudge about how you acquired it."

"Would you care?"

"Depend who it was. What I *do* care about is quality control."

"You take it, test it. You're not happy, we'll renegotiate. We're all businessmen."

Darnell zips up the bag, sets it on the floor. "Go twenty. On account of our history."

"Twenty-five."

"That's high. Let me talk to my boy."

He walks back to the Navigator. Travis waits, his hand near the Ruger.

Darnell comes back with a white paper bag under his arm, the top rolled tight. He gets in, shuts the door. "Told him what you had. He say twenty tops."

"Let's see."

Darnell hands him the bag. Travis opens it, looks at the strapped bills inside, two packs of hundreds.

"Count it," Darnell says.

"No need."

Darnell hefts the knapsack. "When you gonna have some more of that good stuff, the pure?"

"Soon. Getting it together. I'll let you know."

"I heard you had some problems up in the Bricks, with the Ds. A dispute over product."

"You heard wrong."

"True or not, that's the word going around. Heard some people got dropped, too."

"Nothing to do with me."

"Best watch your back anyway," Darnell says. "And let me know on that other thing."

He goes back to the Navigator. Travis looks at the money again. Twenty K, to add to the ten from Jimmy Mac. Good for two hours' work. But not enough.

FOURTEEN

NOAH SETS A folded piece of paper down on the picnic table. "Not a word to anybody where you got this from."

They're sitting in bright sunlight on the concrete patio, the day warm enough that she doesn't need a jacket. He's off duty, in street clothes.

She opens the paper. On it is written *Travis Clay*, with an address in Keansburg and a date of birth that makes him thirty-eight.

"He lied," she says.

"About what?"

"He told me he was commuting all the way from Paterson, not Keansburg. That's only twenty minutes away. Why pay for a motel?"

"That's who the truck's registered to," he says. "Not necessarily the man you met."

"It's him. He came around again yesterday. Told me his name."

"'Came around'? Like stalking you?"

"I don't know if I'd call it that."

"I ran that name. Your instincts were right. He's got a sheet, pulled some time."

"For what?"

"Agg assault. Robbed a dealer, shot him in the leg. Did five years in Rahway. That kind of thing's never a one-off, though. I'm sure he did it before, more than once, just didn't get caught. He's a bad guy. How many times has he come by?"

"Yesterday was the second."

"And he doesn't ask for a room?"

"He says he might, that he's still looking. Said the same the first time."

"He told you that face-to-face?"

"Yeah."

"That's not exactly stalker behavior, being that up-front about it. Usually they're just watchers at first. He ask you out?"

"He did."

"That might be your motivation right there."

She folds the paper, puts it away. "He knew my name. Not sure how. Brianna might have told him, or Baxter."

"You want, I'll go up to Keansburg, see what his deal is."

"That's what I don't want you to do."

"If he's got you worried…"

"Just something about him. And he wanted to pay cash, in advance."

"Not unusual these days. Lot of people ditching their credit cards. Identity theft, data harvesting, all that. Maybe I'll go see him anyway. Rattle his cage a little."

"Don't do that."

"I can convince him to pick another motel, at least. Or take a job in a different county."

"I don't think we're at that point. Chances are he won't be back. I'm just a little jumpy these days."

"You spend too much time alone," he says. "That's part of the problem."

"You could be right."

"Troy wouldn't want that."

She looks at him, unsure how to respond.

He gets up from the table. "This guy shows up again, call me."

"I will. You're a good friend, Noah."

The disappointment on his face fades to a sad smile.

"That's me," he says.

———————

She's restless all day, tries to stay busy. Cara and Brianna are out, so she gets the master key card from the hook in the supply room, lets herself into their unit. She vacuums and dusts, makes the twin beds and leaves fresh towels. At the other rooms, she props open doors to let in fresh air.

With dusk, the temperature drops, the day's warmth only a tease. Driving home, she feels the pull of the Victory, realizes she wants a drink to take the edge off. She wonders if Doreen's working. A shot of Cuervo and a beer might calm her, help her sleep.

Careful with that. If there was ever a time in your life you needed your head on straight, this is it.

The bar's crowded and close, the jukebox loud. Nick, the relief bartender, gives her a wave. She takes the last open stool, can feel men's eyes on her. None of the faces are familiar. She feels out of place, alone. A mistake to come here.

She downs the shot, only finishes half the pint. She leaves a twenty on the bar.

It's a relief to be outside in the cold air again, away from the heat and noise. She's buzzed now, sleepy.

At the trailer, she parks in the carport, steps out into the light. She drops her keys on the steps, feels dizzy as she bends to pick them up. She lets herself in, locks the door behind her. When she turns, Travis Clay is sitting on her couch, half lit by the single lamp.

"I was starting to get worried," he says. "I thought you weren't coming home."

FIFTEEN

S HE FREEZES, SEEING him there in the dimness. Conscious of the
locked door behind her. It would take too long to open.
He'd be on her before she could get out.

He tosses an envelope on the coffee table, flap undone.
The pack of hundreds slides out.

"Sugar jar," he says. "Not that original. All I found,
though, so if there's more hidden around here, you did a
better job of it."

She backs up, bumps the door. *Breathe.*

"What are you doing here?" Aware how foolish it
sounds.

"Go ahead and sit. Let me get a better look at you."

With his foot, he pushes the single chair toward her. She
moves to it slowly, the table between them. He's wearing
gloves.

"Didn't know how long I'd have to wait," he says. "Or if you'd come home alone."

"How did you get in?"

"Nice trailer, but your storm windows are for shit." He cocks his head toward the open bedroom door. "Took me four minutes, tops. Haven't done that in a while, but some things you don't forget. Not very dignified, though, having to crawl through someone's window."

He picks up the photo from the end table. "Who's this? Boyfriend?"

"My husband."

"Where is he?"

"He's dead."

He puts the photo back. "How?"

"Cancer."

"How old was he?"

"He was thirty-five."

"Tough break," he says. "But life's full of them, isn't it? I've seen a lot of good men die in bad ways they didn't deserve."

He brushes sugar crystals from the envelope, takes out the cash. "There was ten grand in this pack. There's eight now. You've been spending my money."

Outside, the carport light clicks off. Everything around her is dark except his face. She can't look away.

"It's like a movie, isn't it?" he says. "Solid citizen gets a wild hair, ends up doing something they shouldn't, thinks they can get away with it. Tommy tell you about the money, or did you find it yourself?"

"He had that envelope on him," she says, testing the lie. "I found it."

"And you figured no one would miss it. Guy's dead or dying, got an envelope full of cash in his pocket, why leave it for some greedy cop? Something like that?"

"Something like that." She thinks of the steak knives in the wooden holder on the kitchenette counter. How far away? Eight feet? Ten? Could she get there before he caught up with her? Does he have a gun?

"Good-enough story," he says. "But I don't believe it. I know what was in that car. We both do. More likely you took it all—or most of it—and hid it somewhere. So you're not such a solid citizen after all."

Her palms are slick. She wipes them on her jeans.

"I admire you, I do," he says. "You played it cool, didn't run, knew that would call attention to you. Right move. I would have found you soon enough anyway. So that tells me you're not stupid. People can get that way when there's a lot of money involved."

He leans forward. "I've been sitting here trying to decide what to do when you showed up, best way to go about it. I was thinking maybe hold your hand on the stove, turn up the burner. Hear what you have to say for yourself then."

Stay calm, she thinks. *If he were going to hurt you, he would have done it already.*

"Part of me wants to put hands on you, pound that pretty face, break a few bones," he says. "That way, every time you look in the mirror you get a reminder of what you did."

He flexes his right hand. She tenses, waiting for him to come at her.

"But that won't get me closer to my money, will it? And then people will ask questions, 'How did your face get so fucked up?' So maybe we can work something out. I get my money, and you get to keep your face."

He puts the cash back in the envelope, slips it in a jacket pocket.

"The temptation there, how it happened? I can see it. Everybody gets to go a little crazy once in their lives. But your fucking thievery has caused me a lot of aggravation, forced me to do things I didn't want to. Give me your cell."

"Why?"

Shut up, she thinks. *Just do what he says.*

She takes the phone from her vest pocket, sets it on the table. He picks it up, taps keys. A phone chirps, muffled, in his jacket pocket. He puts her phone back on the table, slides it toward her.

"I'm going to call you at that number tomorrow, and you're going to answer. Because it's not just you we're talking about."

She has to swallow before she speaks. "What do you mean?"

"That motel you work at? I could burn the whole fucking place down with everybody in it. Wouldn't bother me at all. I'm telling you that so you don't fool yourself into thinking you've got choices. Because you don't."

He stands, and she jerks back in the chair, away from him. He walks past her to the window, looks out through the blinds. "You tell anybody about this?"

"No."

"Good. Because that would be a mistake."

He turns back to her. "And if you do decide to run? Another mistake. Then I have to start looking, asking around, people you know. I'll find you. But those other people will get hurt along the way. And that'll be on you."

Don't say anything. Let him leave.

"Play this right and you'll come out okay. Alive, at least, which is the important part. Maybe a little money for your trouble as well, if I'm feeling generous. You made a wrong decision. It happens. But what you took is mine. Don't ever think different."

He unlocks the door, goes out. The carport light flashes on.

She rushes to the door, locks it. Peering through the blinds, she sees only the Subaru, harshly lit. He's gone.

A sour taste rises fast in her throat. She runs to the bathroom, vomits beer and stomach acid into the bowl. She stays on her knees until the dizziness ends.

When she can stand, she runs water in the sink, drinks from cupped hands, spits, trying to wash away the taste. She can't stop shaking.

Her mattress is half off the bed, the box spring and frame pulled away from the wall. The bureau drawers have been taken out, clothes dumped on the floor. The suitcase is open on its side.

She hears the soft whistle of wind. A draft billows the curtain. The bedroom window is open a crack. She was careless, left it unlocked.

She pushes up the sash. The storm window is missing. She looks out, sees it leaning against the side of the trailer, next to an overturned recycling bucket. He jimmied the window from its frame, set it there, then pried the inner one open and crawled through. *Easy.*

She closes the window, locks it, then sits on the box spring.

If she hadn't left the other money here, if he hadn't found it, he wouldn't have known.

Too late.

SIXTEEN

JOETTE PACES, WATCHES her phone on the desk, waiting for it to ring, hoping it doesn't. Noon, and he still hasn't called. She lay awake most of the night. Now she can't sit still.

The Denali with tinted windows pulls in. She can hear the music inside. Brianna comes out of her room, talks to the driver through his open window. He turns off the engine, gets out, follows her into the office.

"Joette, this is Keith."

He's tall and skinny, wearing a puffy North Face coat, sagging jeans, a white baseball cap, brim to the side, a diamond earring in his left ear.

"I told him all about you," Brianna says. "How cool you've been with us."

He's fidgety, shifting from one foot to the other. He hitches up his pants, puts out his left hand, palm down. Joette looks at it, unsure what to do. He drops his hand, makes a peace sign at waist height.

"I was telling Jo about our plans," Brianna says. "About getting a place."

"Soon as we can," he says. "Just got to get some things wired first."

Brianna puts an arm through his, pulls him close.

He sniffs, says, "I'm gonna bounce, baby girl." He nods at Joette. "Good to meet you." He makes another peace sign at the door.

They watch him get into the Denali. The music's pumping as he pulls away.

"I told you," Brianna says. "He's a good guy. He appreciates what you've done for us."

"I haven't done much."

"I know Singh wanted to put us out. That you talked to him, changed his mind."

"He's just trying to run his business."

"Yeah, but he doesn't care about us, where we might end up. You do. That means a lot. And I know you've got enough to deal with yourself, with your mom and all."

The phone buzzes, makes her jump. It vibrates on the desk. She sees the number, knows who it is.

———

"What are we going to do about this?" he says.

They're sitting on a bench on the Asbury Park boardwalk, facing the empty beach, space between them. Her idea to meet here. She called Singh, told him she was sick, hung the CLOSED sign on the front door and locked it behind her.

The boardwalk kiosks are shuttered for the season, but

a year-round restaurant is open behind them, with big windows that look out on the beachfront.

Nearby, an elderly black man plays an echoey saxophone inside the hollow shell of the old carousel house. She recognizes the tune—"Somewhere Over the Rainbow." Pigeons flutter in the rafters above him. Everything is crystal clear, her senses sharp with fear.

"Normal instinct would be to run," he says. "The fact you didn't, that you're here, tells me you understand the situation."

On the beach, a dog without a leash runs toward a cluster of seagulls. They squawk, spread out and fly off. The dog barks as they circle overhead.

"Was there anyone else involved?" he says.

"No."

"Good. Makes things simpler." He looks out at the waves, massages his knuckles. She can see the spiderweb tattoo.

"You saw an opportunity, took it," he says. "Give you credit for that. Most people wouldn't have the stones. Almost got away with it too."

"I could still go to the police."

"You could, but you won't, or you'd have done it already. And you're not exactly a bystander in all this, are you?"

The wind shifts, comes in cold off the water, makes her shiver. She zips the vest higher. "Some of the money got burned. I'm not sure how much."

"Don't start lying to me now. We both know how much was in there. If any of it burned, there would have been something left over—ashes, bits of bills. Enough for someone to figure out there'd been money in the car. State police didn't find anything."

"If it wasn't for me, it would all be gone. I could have left it in the fire."

"You could have."

"What was it for?" she says.

He looks at her, his face impassive.

"I just want to know, before I give it back," she says.

He looks away. "Let's say it was intended for a purchase that never got made."

"Drugs."

"It was mine, that's all you need to know. You disrupted my life, and that pisses me off. Kept me up last night, thinking about it. Maybe that stove burner wasn't a bad idea after all."

She looks back at the restaurant, the diners inside. She could run, scream, get away from him. But it wouldn't help.

"You're a smart woman," he says. "You didn't just bury that money somewhere. My bet is you took it to a bank, probably more than one. Spread it around."

A jogger thumps by them.

"So you need to gather it all up, wherever it is, whatever you have to do, and bring it to me. Then maybe I let you keep some. Call it a finder's fee, a reward for what you did."

"How much?"

"Off the top of my head? I think one of those packs takes care of that. Say ten thousand."

"Twenty."

He looks at her again. Then he grins, turns away. "Bitch, you are a piece of work."

"For my trouble."

"Get me my money, then we'll talk about it."

"How do I know you won't kill me afterward?"

"You don't. But you don't have much choice, do you?"

She's trying to pretend a calm she doesn't feel. Her left

foot starts to tremble, sneaker tapping on the boards. She can't make it stop.

"I've done time for some things," he says. "But I've gotten away with a lot more. And if they find you somewhere dead, I'll get away with that, too. Because I'm betting there's no one in your life gives a fuck whether you live or die. Am I right?"

She stares straight ahead.

"You're going to call in sick tomorrow," he says. "And then you're going to call me. You'll bring me a list of all the banks you put my money in, and how much in each."

"Then what?"

"Then we go for a ride," he says. "And get it all back."

SEVENTEEN

M AKE THE DEAL," Travis says.

Early morning, and Cosmo looks tired, hungover.
Travis sets the canvas bag on his desk. In it are the twenty
thousand he got from Darnell and the ten from Jimmy
Mac. He kept the eight thousand he found in the woman's
trailer.

Cosmo opens the bag, looks at the banded packs inside. Travis cleaned up the money as best he could. "That
was fast."

"I made some moves."

How much is in here?"

"Thirty K. Add it to the twenty in the pool."

"We're still short."

"Convince them to take the fifty now, front us the
product," Travis says. "Tell them they'll get twenty-five

104

more when we turn it around. That's five thousand over what they asked. They won't argue with that."

"You don't know these guys."

"If they insist on seventy—"

"Oh, they're going to insist. I guarantee."

"—then tell them no deal. We walk. Or they can take the fifty up front, and we hand over the balance as soon as we start selling, plus the bonus. They'll do it if they know there's more cash coming. It's a good bet for them. They know we won't stiff them. If there's a problem later, we're easy to find."

"That supposed to make me feel better?"

"Call them," Travis says. "If you won't take the deal to them, I will. Make the introduction."

"We're taking a risk, going to them with an offer like that. It might just piss them off."

"They won't blow the deal for a few grand. They'd be stupid to do that."

"Maybe so. But I know their reputation. These people are capable of doing something totally fucking outrageous and uncalled-for, just to prove a point."

"So am I," Travis says.

The woman is where she said she'd be, parked in the ShopRite lot off Route 66 in Neptune, next to the clothing collection bins. Across the busy highway is a TD Bank, a stretch of woods behind it.

He drives slow through the lot, checking out the parked cars. Unlikely she called the police, but still a possibility. People don't always think straight when they're scared.

The Subaru's engine is running, exhaust puffing. He

circles the building, drives past tractor-trailers and dumpsters, comes back around. He pulls up alongside her, facing the other direction, lowers his window. Hers is already down.

"That it across the way?" he says.

"That's it. I'll drive over."

He doesn't like the calm in her voice, the confidence. He shifts into park, gets out.

"What are you doing?" she says.

He leans into her window, switches off the ignition, drops the keys in her lap. "Out."

"What's wrong?"

"Get in the fucking truck."

He steps back. She opens the door, gets out slowly. He watches her, ready to head her off if she tries to rabbit.

But if she's planning anything, she's too scared to do it. She climbs in on the truck's passenger side. He gets back behind the wheel.

———

She's trying to stay calm, hide the fear.

"I thought it would be better, drive over there in my own car," she says. "In case anyone there remembers me. It might look suspicious if—"

He grabs her left wrist, jerks it across the console, presses her hand down next to the driver's seat, onto something hard and cold. A gun. "Feel that?"

"Yes."

"So we know where we stand."

When she tries to pull her hand back, he squeezes harder. Pain shoots up her arm. He lets go, and she jerks her hand away, backs up against the door. Her wrist is numb. There are red marks where his fingers were, bright against the paleness of her scars.

"Give me the list."

She takes the folded sheet of notepaper from her vest pocket, hands it to him. On it she's written the names of four banks and dollar amounts.

"You were being careful, weren't you?" he says. "Spreading it around. You open accounts at all of them, or just safe-deposit boxes?"

"Both."

"How much is in the one here?"

"There's an account, but only a few thousand in it. Most of the money's in the safe box. About sixty."

"All hundreds?"

"Yes."

"What were you going to put it in?"

When she doesn't answer, he says, "There's a bag under the seat. You're doing good so far. Don't start fucking up now."

She reaches down, takes out a Kohl's shopping bag, plastic with twine handles.

"You got the keys you need for all the boxes?"

"Yes."

"Your account here, is it checking or savings?"

"Checking."

"How much is in it?"

"Nine thousand."

"You got an ATM card for it?"

"Yes."

"We'll leave that for now. I don't want you staying in there too long. When we're done here, we'll find an ATM, and you'll take out whatever the max is. From the other accounts too. As much as you can until they're dry."

She rubs her wrist. Beneath the bandages, her burns sting for the first time in days. She tries to slow her breathing.

See this through. Get it over with.

"They have security cameras outside the bank too," she says. "The parking lot and drive-through."

"I know. All you need to be concerned about is what you're going to do when you get inside. You open the box, put all the money in that bag, bring it out to me. I count it, then we go to the next bank on that list, do it all again."

He drives to the exit, has to wait for a break in traffic. He pulls out, makes a right, then a sharp left into the half-full bank lot, drives past the building to the edge of the woods. He backs up almost into the trees, facing the bank. She sees the cameras on the side of the building, knows the truck is out of range.

"Look at me," he says.

Her whole body's cold.

"Do what you're supposed to, and we both go home today. But if anything goes wrong at any point? You try to pull some shit, here or someplace else? First thing happens is you get shot in the head. Then I write the rest of the money off to experience, take my chances with the law. Either way, you'll be dead. You understand?"

"Yes."

"Say it."

"I understand."

She looks across the lot to the bank, pictures people on line at the tellers' counter, bank officers in their cubicles. A normal day.

Are you ready for this?

"Good," he says. "Now go get my money."

EIGHTEEN

HER LEGS ARE weak as she crosses the lot. Inside, people are waiting in the two tellers' lines. A row of glass offices, but only one of them is occupied. Inside, a heavyset black man in a suit is talking to a Hispanic couple, the door closed. The nameplate on his desk reads H. BERRY.

She waits in one of the cushioned lobby chairs. The bag is folded under her hoodie, stiff against her side.

The door opens, and the couple comes out with the bank officer. There's an exchange in Spanish she can't follow. When they leave, the bank officer smiles at her and says, "You look like you could use some help."

She shows her driver's license, signs into the logbook. Berry takes her into the vault and uses his master key on her safe box. She goes through her keys to find the right one. Her hand shakes as she fits it into the lock.

"Easy does it," he says. The lock clicks. He slides out the shallow tray, carries it into one of the private coupon booths, sets it on the polished mahogany shelf. "Take your time. Just buzz when you're done." He closes the booth door when he leaves.

Only a week since she's been here, but it feels like a year. She folds back the tray's hinged top. The money is as she left it, six banded packs of hundreds.

She fills her pockets with cash, looks up at the smoke detector on the ceiling. Its green light blinks slowly. She's worked it out in her head, but now she doesn't know if she can go through with it. Then she thinks about Travis Clay out in the truck, waiting for her. The gun.

She pulls out the single chair, takes another sheet of notepaper from her pocket, rolls it into a tube. The chair rocks as she climbs up on it. It creaks under her, and for a moment she thinks it'll collapse.

The Wawa lighter is cheap yellow plastic, but it fires up on the first try. She touches the flame to the paper.

He hears the alarm go off, a steady loud jangling and beeping. Through the windows he can see lights flash inside. There's confusion at first, then people start to mill out onto the sidewalk.

He lifts the Ruger, puts down the passenger window. *You didn't believe me*, he thinks. *You had to test me.*

He inches the truck forward, waiting for her to show

herself, ready to fire through the open window. People cross in front of him.

The sound of a siren close by, sooner than he expected. A police car, rollers flashing, turns into the lot. A secondary siren farther away, a different tempo. Fire truck.

He lowers the gun. When the fire truck pulls in, he drives around it, swings past the police cruiser and pulls out onto the highway.

She's the last customer out of the bank, firefighters rushing past her to get inside. There are two police cars in the lot now. More sirens warble in the distance.

His truck is gone.

Her pockets are bulky with money. She left the shopping bag behind in the booth. No one seems to notice as she moves away from the crowd and into the woods.

Driving, he fumbles with his phone, speed-dials her number. He's been making a circuit, up the highway, then around a jug handle and back again on the other side, watching for her. Firefighters and cops are still standing around outside the bank.

After six rings there's no answer, no voice prompt. He throws the phone at the dashboard. It bounces off and lands on the floor.

Her cell buzzes. His number. She's at the other end of the woods, looking out on a mall parking lot. He'll be driving around, looking for her. Safer to stay here for now.

She sits on a log, catches her breath. The phone keeps buzzing. She shuts it off.

———

"Pull up here," she says. The taxi steers to the curb in front of the ShopRite.

It's dark out. She spent an hour in the trees, then crossed the mall lot to the theater, picked a movie at random. She took a seat in the back, gradually drifted into sleep as the adrenaline wore off. She woke when the lights came up, went back into the lobby and bought a ticket for a different film. She stayed awake for most of it but remembers almost nothing.

The Subaru is still there at the other end of the supermarket lot. The police presence at the bank would have driven him away, but for how long? Is he somewhere nearby, watching the car?

The driver is a middle-aged black woman in a yachting cap. She looks at Joette in the rearview. "What are we doing, honey? I've got other calls."

"That's my car there by the clothing bins. Can you drive over, but take it slow?"

She stays low in the seat, scans the lot as they cross it. As they near the Subaru, she sees the tires are flat, the chassis low to the ground.

"If that's your car, you need to call the police," the driver says. "Someone did that on purpose."

"Can we just wait here a few minutes?"

"You in some kind of trouble?"

"A little bit."

"And you don't want the police?"

"No," Joette says.

She takes a breath, trying to brace herself.

He's gone. You pulled it off. Now go get what's yours.

She gets out, keys in hand, walks quickly to the Subaru. All four tires have puncture marks in the sidewalls. She opens the trunk, pulls out her suitcase, shuts the lid. There's nothing else in the car she needs.

Back in the cab, the suitcase beside her, she says, "Can you get someone else to take those calls?"

"Why?"

She takes two hundreds from her jeans pocket, leans forward and holds them out.

"I need to find a place to stay. A motel. The farther away the better."

The driver takes the bills.

"They're real," Joette says.

"I see that. How far do you want to go?"

"As far as they'll take me," she says.

NINETEEN

AT NINE O'CLOCK, he's parked alongside the dark restaurant on Route 35, cell phone on the seat beside him. He's had three calls from Cosmo, hasn't answered them or listened to the messages.

He puts on the gloves, gets out. He follows the same path as last time, scales the fence, staying in the shadow of the trees. The windows of her trailer are dark, the carport empty. All he can hear is the low murmur of a television from the trailer next door.

He listens under her bedroom window. No sound inside.

The recycling bucket's gone, but there's a cinder block in the crawl space under the trailer. He drags it out, stands on it to look through the gap in the curtains. The bed's unmade, the closet door ajar. The dresser drawers are back in place.

He takes out his tactical knife, opens the five-inch blade.

The storm window comes out easily again. He leans down and sets it against the side of the trailer.

The inner sash is locked this time, as he expected. Closing the knife, he takes the roll of black electrician's tape from his jacket, tears off strips and presses them against the glass just above the twist lock. Three horizontal lines crossed with an X.

He pops the butt of the knife sharply against the X until the glass cracks. Shards of it come away as he peels off the tape, leaving a gap big enough to reach through. He folds the tape on itself, tosses it lightly onto the ground, puts away the knife. With his left hand, he reaches in, feels for the lock, his wrist at an awkward angle.

Pain slices across his middle finger. He yanks his hand back. Blood begins to ooze from a horizontal cut through the glove. He looks in at an angle, and he can see the razor blade wedged into the base of the twist lock. That bitch.

He reaches through with his right hand, careful to avoid the blade. It's single-edged, so he can grasp it at its metal base, work it back and forth until it comes loose. He drops it inside, then undoes the lock, pushes up the sash. His gloved finger leaves a bloody smear on the frame.

Inside, he draws the Ruger. The trailer is quiet, empty. The suitcase is gone.

In the bathroom, he sets the gun on the toilet tank, turns on the light. The glove is slick with blood. He pulls it off, runs water over his finger. The puckered edges of the cut are white for an instant, then red again.

He fumbles with a tin of bandages from the medicine cabinet. Two of them cover the wound. He pulls the glove back on, but there's blood everywhere, drops of it on the sink and floor.

There's enough light coming through that he can see his

way around the darkened trailer. All the windows have razor blades in their locks. On the kitchenette counter, an open package of Red Devil blades, gleaming and new.

A wicker basket hangs on the kitchen wall. Inside are an electric bill, a balance-due notice—$350—for a brake job on the Subaru. More bills. An open envelope with the return address of *Kingsley Gardens Care Facility* in Galloway Township, an hour south. There's a form letter inside, a notification for a Care Plan Meeting earlier that week. The resident's name—Irene Kelly—and the time and date have been filled in with blue ink. He folds the letter, pockets it.

No sense searching the trailer again. She'll have taken any money with her.

He opens cabinets until he finds what he's looking for beneath the sink, a full pint can of paint thinner. It'll do. He carries it back into the bedroom, splashes thinner on the bed, then in a trail to the living room. He notices that the photo from the end table is gone.

He empties the can onto the furniture, tosses it on the couch, takes a skillet down from the kitchen wall. He fills it with cooking oil, turns the stove burner on high. It's close enough to the window that the curtains will catch easily. The oil is already smoking when he lets himself out the front door. The light clicks on above him.

"What are you doing in there?"

A woman stands in the carport holding a cell phone. She's wearing a sweat suit. Her gray hair is tied back in a ponytail.

He smiles. "I'm looking for Joette. Have you seen her?"

"Who are you?"

"A friend of hers. She was supposed to meet me here."

"I'm going to call the police."

"You don't need to do that. She gave me a key. Did I miss her? How long ago did—"

A crackling behind him, a flare of light in the kitchenette window. The curtains going up.

The woman punches keys on the phone. He takes out the Ruger, points it at her. "Don't do that." His finger's on the trigger. "Let it fall."

The phone clatters on the concrete. Lights go on in another trailer. A dog begins to bark.

"Back away," he says.

When she does, he steps hard on the phone, kicks the pieces aside. Behind him, orange light flickers in the trailer windows. Glass pops and cracks.

He backs away into the trees, the woman watching him. At the fence, he pockets the Ruger, climbs over.

When he reaches the truck, he looks back. There's a red glow and a plume of smoke over the trailer park, sparks rising up.

Close this time. He almost got caught. He underestimated her twice today. It won't happen again.

———

The motel is two miles outside Atlantic City, looking out across acres of salt marsh. On the horizon, the high-rise casino hotels glow against the dark sky, a neon Oz. An hour-and-a-half drive down here. She gave the driver another two hundred.

She splashes water on her face at the sink, looks in the mirror at the deeper crow's-feet, the tightness around her eyes from lack of sleep.

Her suitcase is open on the bed, the money inside, along with everything she brought from the trailer.

There it is. Your whole life in total.

She takes out the framed picture of her and Troy on the river, props it up on the dresser. The only photo she took with her.

Their wedding bands are in a gray ring box. She can't remember the last time she wore hers, but she couldn't leave them behind. She opens the box, sets it in front of the photo. All that's left of what they once were. Her engagement ring was pawned long ago, against that first wave of medical bills. She never told him.

Her cell vibrates on the bed. His number again. She answers this time, opens the line, hears muted traffic sounds.

"That was pretty swift back at the bank," he says. "You see that in a movie? The razor blades too?"

Siren noise coming through.

"Hear that?" he says. "No false alarm this time."

"What did you do?"

"You're running me around a little, I get that. Wouldn't feel right giving it up without a fight. But some point soon, you're going to realize it isn't worth it. You'll be begging me to take it back."

The sirens grow fainter.

"What made you think you could keep it, anyway?" he says. "Made you think that was ever a possible outcome?"

She looks at herself in the dresser mirror, the lines in her face. "I don't know. I guess I just got tired of people taking things away from me."

He starts to speak. She powers down the phone, watches it go dark.

TWENTY

SHE SLEEPS FITFULLY, no more than two hours at a time. At dawn, she stands at the window and watches the sun rise over the salt marsh, lighting up the glass towers of the distant casinos floor by floor.

A taxi takes her to the local Enterprise office, where she rents a Honda Civic. She buys a disposable phone at a drugstore, calls Brianna's cell and leaves a message. On the way back to the motel, she stops on a low bridge, tosses her old phone into the water below.

She's in her room when Brianna calls back.

"Joette, are you okay? The cops are here, talking to Baxter. They said something about a fire at your trailer."

The sirens.

"You and Cara need to get your things together, get out of there. Is there someplace you can go?"

"Why? What's wrong?"

"Can you stay with your mother?" Joette says. "If not, find another motel. I'll pay for it. But you need to get away from there, soon as you can. Don't tell anyone where you're going."

"I don't understand."

"I don't have time to explain it all now. Listen to me, Bree, please."

"What about Singh?"

"I paid you up for the month. You don't owe him anything. Just get out of there."

"You got me worried now."

"I'll check back with you in a couple hours. In the meantime, ask Keith to call me at this number. But don't let anyone else know you talked to me. Not even the police."

"You're scaring me."

"Don't be scared," Joette says. "Just go."

———

She watches Keith's Denali come down the ramp into the casino parking garage. He's an hour late. She flashes the Honda's lights.

He pulls into a space opposite her. She gets out, walks over. He unlocks the passenger door.

"You a gambler?" he says when she gets in.

"No."

"Then what are we doing all the way down here?"

"Are Bree and Cara safe?"

"They're at her mom's house in Howell. She's visiting Bree's sister down in Alabama, so she's been away. We did what you asked, but I still don't know why."

"You bring something for me?" she says.

"We need to talk about that."

"You didn't?"

"You gonna tell me what you need it for?"

"Protection."

"From who? You want a gun, get a license. Then go down to Walmart, buy any kind of gun you want."

"I don't want a license," she says. "And I don't want anything that's traceable."

"Traceable? What are you into here? And why did you ask me?"

"I thought you could help. Was I wrong?"

He reaches under his seat, comes up with an oil-spotted brown paper bag. "Keep it low."

She opens the bag, takes out the gun. It's a small flat automatic, blue steel and wood grips. The sheen is dull, and one of the grips is cracked. She's never held a pistol before. It feels light in her hand, more a toy than a weapon.

"Colt twenty-five," he says. "Careful, it's loaded. You know anything about guns?"

She shakes her head.

"This one's good for you. Doesn't kick or make much noise."

He takes the gun, pushes a lever on the butt and slips out the clip, shows her the shiny brass bullets inside. "Six rounds in there."

"What if I need more?"

"You're on your own with that." He pushes the clip back in until it locks.

"You tell Bree about this?" she says.

"No."

"Don't. What's that on the side?"

"Slide lock. It's a safety. Keep it on until you're ready to fire. There's a grip safety too, so you have to hold the gun tight when you squeeze the trigger."

He draws back the slide halfway, shows her the empty chamber.

"Nothing in there now. But when you do it all the way"—he pulls the slide back farther, and a bullet rises into position—"then a round pops in."

He lets the slide snap closed.

"With one in the chamber and the safety off, you're good to go. All you have to do is pull the trigger. It's small-caliber, though. You shoot something, best keep shooting until you run out of bullets."

He hands her back the gun. Holding it, she wonders if she's making a mistake. Doing something there's no coming back from.

She clicks the slide lock on, then off again. "How much?"

"Five hundred."

"That's too much."

"Like you know how much it's worth?" he says. "Or what I had to do to get it this fast?"

"Two hundred." Pulling the number out of the air.

"Price is five," he says. "You asked. I delivered. You don't want it, you don't want it."

She puts the gun back in the bag, sets it on the console. "Thanks anyway. Sorry you had to make the trip." She opens the door.

"Wait a minute."

She looks at him.

"You got it with you?" he says.

She pulls the door closed, takes the hundreds from her vest pocket, peels off two, sets them on the console.

"On second thought," he says. "Whatever you need it for, I don't want to know about it."

"I have something for Brianna, too." She takes the check from her shirt pocket. "It's for her and Cara, help them get settled. It's made out to her, she can cash it at my bank. Tell her if she needs more, to call me. And tell her I'm sorry about all this, what I put them through."

He takes the check, unfolds it. "A thousand? For real?"

"Real enough," she says. She picks up the bag, opens the door. "Take care of them."

———————

Back in the room, she sits on the edge of the bed, unloads the gun again, trying to get a feel for it. She pulls the slide back, and the chambered bullet pops out. She pushes it back into the clip.

Is this what you've become? Someone who carries a gun?

Standing in front of the mirror, she slips the clip back into the gun, thumbs on the safety. When she slides the gun into her right front jeans pocket, it's barely visible.

If it comes down to it, will you be able to pull the trigger?

She doesn't know the answer.

TWENTY-ONE

"WE BLEW IT," Cosmo says.

They're headed south on the Turnpike in the Lexus, Cosmo at the wheel.

"What do you mean?" Travis says. He's distracted, thinking about the Harper woman, what she might do next. Wondering where she got the nerve to take it as far as she had.

"We should have been investing that fent money, those first big paydays we had," Cosmo says. "Moved on to other things."

"Like what?"

"Real estate. Residential properties. Luxury apartments for foreigners who need to hide their cash over here. We would have tripled our investment by now, left all this other mess behind."

"Little late for that. What do you know about real estate, anyway?"

"Enough to know we should be thinking bigger. The money we lost, that three hundred grand? That's nothing. These hedge fund guys, investment bankers, they make that at lunch. And nobody gets shot."

Travis flexes his left hand. The cut finger itches beneath the bandages. There's a dark spot where it's started to bleed through. "How much farther?"

"Exit's coming up. It's a couple more miles from there. I hope you've been listening to me."

"I have. Real estate."

"Once we get the bank back up, we should do that. Invest. Stop screwing around with lowlifes. We can work it the same way we always did. Start off with seed money and build."

"And nobody gets hurt," Travis says.

"That's right. Think about it. We can still do it."

They take the exit, drive for another mile, then turn onto a two-lane road, pine forest on both sides. Their headlights illuminate a rusted sign that says MUNICIPAL AIRPORT, with the silhouette of a plane, and an arrow pointing ahead.

A chain-link fence runs along on the right. Through gaps in the trees, Travis can see a clearing beyond.

Cosmo slows. "There should be a gate up ahead."

"Pull over."

"Here? Why?"

"Do it. Kill the lights, open the back."

Cosmo steers onto the shoulder, dims the headlights. Travis gets out, leaves the door open. He pulls on gloves, waits for the rear hatch to rise, takes out the knapsack with the fifty thousand. Under the wheel well is the Ruger. He fits the gun into his belt, shuts the hatch.

He sets the knapsack on the passenger seat. "You're taking it."

"What?"

"You're bringing the money to them. Tell them I punked out, got scared."

"They're expecting both of us."

"The money's there. That's all they care about."

"I already pissed these guys off when I told them we were only bringing fifty. I change up on them again, they're not gonna be happy."

"You're here to give them the money, pick up the product. That's what you're going to do."

"What about you?"

"I'll be close by. Do what they say, stay cool, it'll be fine."

"Why didn't you tell me this before?"

"Didn't want to give you too much time to worry about it, get nervous."

"Jesus, thanks a lot."

"Go on."

Travis watches the Lexus drive away, headlights on. Farther down the road it slows again, makes a right turn through an open gate.

He walks the fence line until he comes to a spot where the chain-link sags almost to the ground. He climbs over it, makes his way up a gradual slope into the woods. When he reaches the far edge of the trees, he's looking down on the airport. A half-moon shines above.

A concrete hangar is the only building left on the cracked tarmac. Its big front doors are shut, light creeping out around their edges. There's a metal side door. Next to it, a window throws a square of light on the ground.

Cosmo pulls up to the doors. One of them slides open, pushed by someone within. Travis can see two motorcycles and an SUV inside. The Lexus drives through, the door closing behind it.

Branches rustle. He smells the sharp tang of cigarette smoke. More rustling, then the glow of a cigarette that flares and fades.

There are two men about ten feet ahead of him, sitting on the ground, watching the hangar. The smoker is to his left. In the moonlight, Travis can see he has long hair, a beard, is wearing a sleeveless denim jacket over leather. The man on the right is hidden in shadow.

The Ruger would be too loud here. He takes out the tactical knife, folds open the blade.

The second man stands.

"What are you doing?" the biker says. "Sit your ass down."

"I want to see." A Latin accent. "I have my reasons."

"Fuck your reasons. We're supposed to stay here."

"This is personal."

He starts down the slope, moving loudly through the brush. He crosses the tarmac, knocks at the side door. It opens, spilling light, and he goes in.

Better odds now. Travis grips the knife like an icepick, blade pointing down. He slows his breath, steadying himself, moves closer. The biker flicks his cigarette away. He's sitting on a log, a pump shotgun across his knees.

A cloud crosses the moon. Travis slaps a hand across the man's mouth, pulls him back and stabs him in the chest, four, five, six times, fast as he can, aiming for the heart. The man tries to twist away, and Travis stabs him twice more, quick and deep, turning the blade. It scrapes on bone as he yanks it free.

He shoves the man away, leaves him whimpering face-down in the dirt, bleeding out. He wipes the slick blade on the man's denim jacket, then closes the knife and puts it away.

Sitting on the log, he picks up the shotgun, brushes off dirt and pine needles. The barrel and stock have been sawn down. He works the pump to eject the rounds into his lap. Seven shells, a mix of twelve-gauge buck and solid lead deer slugs.

He blows into the receiver to clear it, then feeds the shells back in, leading with a slug. He cycles the pump to chamber a round. Cut down like it is, there's not much weight to the gun. It'll kick hard.

He looks at the hangar, wondering what they're doing to Cosmo in there, what he's telling them.

Ten long breaths, and he's ready. He stands, walks down the slope, cuts across the tarmac and crouches outside the window. He can hear the muffled thump and hum of a generator inside.

He raises up, looks in. Cosmo is bound to a wooden chair in the middle of the floor, duct tape on his fore-arms and calves. A Dominican sits facing him, almost knee to knee. Nearby is a makeshift table, a sheet of plywood across two sawhorses. On it are a stainless steel revolver, a pair of pruning shears and the knap-sack.

Three other men in the room. A biker stands by the motorcycles, arms crossed, watching. The Dominican from the woods is behind Cosmo's chair. Another Dominican waits by the side door.

The seated man is older than the others. Chano's age. He says something Travis can't hear, taps Cosmo on the knee. Cosmo shakes his head. The man leans closer and slaps him hard across the face.

Cosmo turns his face away, waiting for another blow.

The Dominican stands, goes to the table and picks up the shears.

Travis bangs twice on the door with the bottom of his fist. "Open up. Got some trouble out here." Keeping his voice flat.

From the other side, *"¿Qué?"*

"Open the door."

He backs up, aims the shotgun chest high. When he hears a lock turn, he squeezes the trigger. The stock kicks back, and the slug blows a quarter-sized hole through the metal. He pumps, fires, twelve-gauge this time, a wide spray that sends the door back on its hinges. He pumps again, goes through.

There's a man at his feet, chest shiny with blood. Travis steps over him, moves fast to the left, away from the door. The Dominican drops the shears, reaches for the pistol.

Travis fires, the sound echoing off the high ceiling. The Dominican twists with the impact of the buckshot, loses the pistol. The biker dives to the floor.

Travis swings the shotgun toward Cosmo, racks it. "Down."

Cosmo throws himself to the side, topples the chair, exposing the man behind him. Travis hits the Dominican in the chest with a round of buckshot, knocks him off his feet.

The biker is up, running for the open side door. Travis fires over his head. The biker pulls up short, hands raised. Travis gestures him back toward the motorcycles.

The wounded Dominican is crawling toward his revolver, trailing blood on the concrete. Travis circles him, kicks the gun away and fires into his back. He racks the shotgun again. A smoking shell rolls across the floor.

"Hey, man," the biker says. "This ain't got nothing to do with me."

"Get on the floor."

The biker kneels. "No lie. I didn't know what was going down here."

"All the way. Hands behind your head."

To Cosmo, Travis says, "You hit?"

"I don't think so. Cut me loose."

Travis goes to him, flicks open the knife. There are spots of blood on Cosmo's face. His crotch is wet.

Travis saws through the duct tape on his right arm, gives him the knife. "You can do the rest."

He squats in front of the biker. "What's your name?" The generator chugs away behind them.

"Val."

"Val, you want to tell me what went on here?"

Cosmo pulls the last of the tape off his legs. He's shaky getting up. "I can tell you what went on."

"I want to hear it from this guy."

"It was all the Dominicans," the biker says. "It was their deal."

"Explain."

"They came to us, said you might be asking around, looking to buy. They wanted us to get you down here, said we could keep whatever cash you brought. We didn't know what they were planning to do."

"You had an idea." He stands, kicks the pruning shears toward the biker. "What were you gonna do, stand around and watch?"

He goes to the table, opens the knapsack, looks at the banded bills inside. "You take any of this?"

"No," the biker says. "It's all there."

Cosmo has righted the chair, is sitting with his head in his hands, the open knife on the floor at his feet.

"You okay?" Travis says.

"Yeah. I just want to get out of here before I get sick."

"I didn't have anything to do with this," the biker says. "I just came along for the ride. I got nothing against you."

Travis walks over to him. "You think I'm not going to kill you?"

"Man, I fucking *know* you're going to kill me. So I've got nothing to lose, right? That's how you know I'm telling the truth."

"Makes sense. Thing is, though, you sold us out, set us up."

"It wasn't me, man."

Travis points the shotgun at his head. "Close your eyes."

"*Wait!*"

Travis fires. The sound echoes through the hangar. Cosmo looks away.

Travis sets the gun on the table, zips up the knapsack, slings it over his shoulder.

"Get sick later," he says. "We need to go."

———

Travis drives. Cosmo looks out the window, trembles every once in a while, as if with a chill. He hasn't spoken since they left the hangar.

"You did good in there," Travis says. "You gonna be okay?"

"Why'd you send me in alone?"

"I wanted to have a look around, in case it was a setup. Good thing, too. What did they ask you?"

"What do you think they asked me? Where you were. Why you weren't there. I said what you told me to. I don't think they believed it."

"You gave me the time I needed."

"They were going to cut off my fingers."

"But they didn't."

Travis lowers the window, feels the cold air on his face.

"Look at it this way," he says. "There were five men back there, waiting to kill us. Fucking Valley of Death, and we walked out of it without a scratch. We're the kings of the jungle tonight, man. Believe it."

TWENTY-TWO

MORNING, AND SHE'S parked down the street from the trailer, her hoodie pulled up. She doesn't want neighbors to see her.

Crime scene tape is strung across the warped front door. All the windows are gone, the walls around them dark with soot. The carport is full of debris and blackened furniture. The smell of smoke and damp hangs in the air. Part of her wants to tear off the tape, go inside and see what's left.

That's your old life. There's nothing for you there now. Anything you find will only hurt.

She takes out her cell phone, considers calling Noah, telling him she's all right. He'll hear about the fire eventually, will come looking for her. It would complicate things. First she needs a plan.

Or you could just tell him. Turn the money over to the police. Take the consequences, whatever they are. One call and it's all over.

She puts the phone down, watches the crime scene tape flutter in the wind.

———————

Her mother is asleep in her room when Joette gets to the nursing home. She's propped up on pillows, tiny and frail beneath the covers. The bed rails are locked in place on each side.

There's a game show on the wall-mounted TV, the volume muted. The only sound is chatter from the nurses' station down the hall, the trundle of a medication cart.

She brings a chair close, watches her mother breathe, the sheet barely moving. She takes her hand, feels the bones just beneath the skin.

There's a light knock at the open door. Kimberly, the day nurse, is there.

"Your mom wasn't feeling very well this morning. She only ate a little breakfast, so I decided to put her back in bed, let her rest. I've been keeping an eye on her."

"Thank you."

"You look tired."

"A long couple days. How is she doing?"

"Her vitals are still strong. She just can't seem to stay awake very long."

"I'll be here for a while," Joette says. "If they bring a tray in for lunch, I'll try to feed her."

"I'll let them know. I'm just down the hall if you need me."

Joette brushes a lock of hair from her mother's eyes, listens to her faint breathing.

Where are you, Mom? What are you dreaming? Who do you see?

She feels a slight squeeze on her hand, not sure at first if she's only imagined it. It comes again, weaker this time. *She knows you're here.*

She kisses her mother's forehead. "I've got to go away for a while, Mom," she whispers. "But I'll be back soon. I promise."

She takes her mother's hand in both of hers, holds it tight.

She calls him from the parking lot. The line buzzes seven times, stops. She disconnects, then calls again. This time he picks up.

"We can make a deal," she says.

"Too late."

"No deal, no money."

"What money would that be?"

"You're worried about the phone. Don't be. I just bought it."

"Smart. Sometimes, though, smart people overplay their hands. Because they're not as smart as they think they are."

"I just want this to end. You were right. I have too much to lose."

"And how do you see it ending?"

"You lost something. I found it. Now we can talk about how much you're willing to let me keep."

"That offer's closed."

"You need me, or you get nothing. That list I gave you—"

"Is bogus, yeah. I figured that out. That stunt at the bank didn't solve anything, though. All it did was make me angry. Tell me, how long had you planned that? Known what you were gonna do?"

"Not long. And I lost my trailer, so we're even."

"We're not even close to even. Curious, is Irene Kelly your mother, or grandmother? Mother, I bet. And Kingsley Gardens isn't that far away, is it?"

The back of her neck goes cold. "Stay away from there."

"That's what I mean by overplaying your hand. Way I see it, all you've put me through, anything happens now is fair game."

It must have been something she left behind in the trailer. Something he found before he set the fire.

Don't panic. She's safe there. No one can just walk in past security. No way he can get to her. It's a bluff.

"Ask yourself how far you want to take this," he says. "Because I can take it all the way. You want to spiral with me, babe, I'm good with that."

"I have the sixty from the first bank. I'll hand it over to you. Then we can talk about the rest."

"Nothing to talk about. We take a ride, get *all* the money from *all* the banks. One shot. That's it."

"Then what happens?"

"That'll be up to me," he says. "And I haven't decided yet."

———————

Driving back to Atlantic City, she calls Helen, puts her on speakerphone. "I need a favor," Joette says. "A big one."

"Hold on. Let me take this in the break room."

Joette hears voices, then a door opening and closing, muting the noise.

"This is bad, isn't it?" Helen says.

"I got involved in something I shouldn't have." She's fighting a rising panic, trying to focus, think it through. "But I might know a way out."

"Talk to me."

"The less I tell you right now, the better."

"I don't like the sound of that."

"I may have to leave town for a while."

"What's 'a while'?"

"I don't know yet."

"What about your mother?"

"I just need you to look in on her every few days, see how she's doing. I was just there. I dropped off a check that'll cover us for three months."

"How'd you come up with that kind of money?"

"I took a gamble on something. It paid off."

"And that's why you have to leave town?"

"It might not be for long. I need someone back here I can trust. And I wanted to tell you that I was going, so you wouldn't worry."

"Not worry? No chance of that."

"Please, Helen. I need your help. Otherwise, I have nobody."

A pause. "This is a lot to process," Helen says. "When are you leaving?"

"Maybe tomorrow."

"That's not much warning. But I can't say no."

"You can. I'd understand."

"No, I can't. But, girl, what did you get yourself into?"

"It'll be done soon," Joette says. "One way or another."

———

"I'm done," Cosmo says. "I'm out."

They're in the apartment over the hardware store. Travis is at the window, looking down on the night-dark street. Cosmo's at the kitchen table.

"Hate to hear you say that," Travis says. "After all this time."

"That was fucked up down there. Things just keep getting worse. Maybe it's time to shut it all down."

Travis goes to the refrigerator, takes out two Heinekens, opens them on the breakfast counter. "You're disappointing me, brother, all we've been through. What did you do with the fifty?"

"It's in the safe at my place, along with the last of the fent. Listen, T. Buying and selling is one thing. That's business. But what's going on now…"

Travis sets a beer in front of him. "We did what we had to do."

"How many people do we have looking for us now? We're worse off than when we started. Nothing to sell, and not enough money to make a buy. It's time to quit. You can keep the fifty. I'm through."

"Give it some time. You might see things differently. I talked to Darnell Jackson today. Anything we can get, he'll take. We find another seller, buy as much as we can, offload it all to Darnell, double our money. You want to walk then, go ahead. But at least both of us will have a stake."

"I just want to go back to the way things were."

"I'll have some more cash on hand soon too. Keep us going for a while."

"From where?"

"Someone that owes me. It'll get us back in the game."

"I don't know," Cosmo says. He picks up the beer but doesn't drink.

"Find a connect," Travis says. "Wherever you have to go. We make one last buy, sell it off, go our separate ways with a nice little nest egg for each of us, if that's what you want."

"You think it'll be that easy?"

"Why not?" Travis says.

TWENTY-THREE

H E'S WAITING FOR her in the bank lot, parked near the exit. She pulls in behind his truck. They're at the PNC in Toms River, the first bank she left money in, a hundred years ago. Nine a.m. and the lot filling up.

He leaves the truck, walks back to the Honda. She unlocks the passenger door. He's wearing the brown work jacket, gloves.

He gets in, nods at the shoulder bag on the floor. "That for me?"

"Sixty grand. It's all there."

"Where did you get the car?"

"It's a rental."

He opens the bag, sorts through the packs, thumbs bills. "Looks right. How much in the safe box here?"

"Another sixty."

He puts the money back, zips up the bag.

"I'm going in," she says. "I want to get this over with."

"In a minute."

He reaches under the jacket, and then there's a gun in his hand. He pushes it hard into her armpit, twists it. The pain lifts her out of her seat.

"One shot at this range, almost no noise," he says. "Nobody hears anything. Nobody sees anything. I get out of the car, walk away, and Avis gets to clean up the mess."

He moves the gun to his left hand, reaches over to pat her vest pockets, her waist, her stomach. His hand passes quickly over her breasts, then around to the small of her back. Finally to her thighs, down the inside of each leg to her ankles.

"I'm not wired," she says. "You can put that away. I'll get your money."

He puts the gun in his jacket pocket. Her armpit is sore. She takes a breath, can't seem to fill her lungs.

"Go on," he says. "Leave the engine running."

She reaches down for the bag. He catches her wrist.

"It's all fifties in that box," she says. "They'll take up a lot of room. I'll need something to put them in."

He holds her arm for a moment, then lets go. She takes the bag, slings the strap over her shoulder, gets out. Crossing the lot, harsh sunlight flashes off the bank windows, blinds her.

A woman bank manager lets her into the vault. Together they key the lock. Joette slides the box out, takes it into the privacy booth, shuts the door behind her.

———————

When she leaves the bank, the bag heavier, he's behind the wheel of the Honda. She hesitates, then gets in on the passenger side.

"Show me," he says.

She opens the bag, tilts it toward him so he can see the money. "You want to count it?"

"Not here."

"I could have called the police," she says. "Told them you were out here, that you had a gun."

"But you didn't."

"I just want this over. And you out of my life."

"Almost. Tell me where we're going."

"The Wells Fargo on Route Thirty-Five in Ocean Township. Head east toward the Parkway. I'll show you."

He pulls out of the lot. She rubs a palm on her jeans leg.

This was always the way it would go, she thinks. When he has all the money, he'll take her somewhere, shoot her, dump the car.

You know what you have to do.

"I think I'm going to be sick," she says.

"Forget it."

"I'm serious. I've been nauseous all morning. I feel like I'm going to throw up."

"Hold it in."

"I can't."

"You have to. We're not stopping."

"You want me to do it in the bank, while I'm getting your money?"

He looks at her. She winces. "Cramps."

"Don't throw up in the car."

"Then you better stop."

She sees the empty lot coming up on the left, woods surrounding it. There was an Italian ice stand there years ago. The building's long gone, nothing in its place.

"Pull in there," she says. "Quick. Please."

He slows, has to wait for oncoming traffic before he

steers into the lot. It's overgrown, the blacktop cracked. She knows there's a shallow creek that runs behind the trees.

He pulls to the rear of the lot. From here, she can see the slope. It's littered with trash and shiny wet leaves.

"Stay there," he says. He gets out, goes around to her door, opens it. "Get out."

When she doesn't move, he grabs her upper arm, pulls her from the car. His other hand is in the pocket with the gun.

He shuts the door, pushes her toward the trees. "Straight ahead, and be quick about it. I'm right behind you. Try to run, and I'll put one in your back."

He shoves her again. She stumbles, nearly falls. They're almost in the shadows of the trees.

"I should pop you right now," he says. "Make it simpler for both of us."

Her right hand goes into her vest pocket, curls around the butt of the .25 she took from the safe box. Her finger slides across the trigger. The safety is already off.

"Hurry up," he says. "What are you—"

She pulls at the gun. It catches on her pocket, then comes out all at once. She brings it up as she turns toward him. He's already backstepping, surprise in his face.

Do it.

The gun jumps in her hand. The bullet goes past him, snaps bark off a tree. His own gun comes out, and she fires again in panic, sees the bullet hit his left shoulder, turn him. He throws himself to the side, tries to swing his gun back toward her, and then his foot slides out from under him on the wet earth. He loses his balance, falls backward down the slope, fires once into the air.

Move.

She runs to the car, gets behind the wheel, tosses the .25

on the passenger seat. She can hear him fighting his way back up through the underbrush.

She shifts into reverse, foot on the gas. He's at the top of the bank now. She hears the crack of his gun, floors the gas and spins the wheel. Then she's out on the highway, swerving to miss an oncoming car, oversteering. Horns blare around her.

Her last sight of him is in the rearview. He's standing on the shoulder, the gun down at his side, watching as she drives away.

———

Forty minutes later, she pulls into a Target off the north-bound Parkway, steers the Honda to the far side of the lot, away from the highway. She opens the door and vomits, thin and watery, onto the ground.

You tried to kill a man.

She wonders how badly he was hurt, if the bullet did much damage. It didn't stop him, or even slow him down. Until she drew her gun, she didn't know if she'd have the courage to aim at him, fire. She hesitated, finger on the trigger, and then it all happened so fast.

Keep going. Stick with the plan

She opens the trunk, pulls off the blanket covering her suitcase. Inside is the cash she took from the other two banks the day before. She adds the money from the shoulder bag, zips the suitcase shut. All the cash in one place now. She closes the trunk.

She feels strangely calm, with tasks ahead of her, some-where to go. She'll leave the car at Penn Station in Newark. Ditch her phone and get a new one. Buy her Amtrak ticket with cash.

TWENTY-FOUR

YOU NEED A doctor," Cosmo says.

"Just hold it still, goddammit."

Travis is shirtless at his kitchen table. Cosmo is holding up his iPhone, the video camera reversed. On the screen, Travis can see the entry wound in his shoulder, two inches from his collarbone.

"It was a piece-of-shit twenty-five," he says. "It's in there against the muscle, didn't go any deeper. I can feel it."

In front of him on a white bath towel are a pair of tweezers, his knife, an open bottle of alcohol, a packet of gauze pads, surgical tape and a coffee mug. Another towel in his lap.

He splashes alcohol from the bottle onto the wound. The clotting washes away and blood begins to flow.

"I don't know how you can do this," Cosmo says.

Travis pours alcohol into the mug, dips in the tweezers.

He grabs the handcuff chain, hauls the cop to his feet. He's wobbly, red-faced. Travis pushes him toward the counter.

"That her plan, send you after me? What am I supposed to do with you now, position you put me in?"

"Let me go."

Travis kicks his feet apart, forcing him to lean against the counter to keep his balance. He pats the cop's pockets, finds a cell phone and a key fob, tosses them onto the counter. "You banging her? That what this is about? You think you're going to protect her? You can't."

He looks out the window. Still no backup, but someone may have heard the shot. Either way, the apartment's no good now, he can't stay here. He feels a wave of anger at this stupid cop, the damage he's done.

He puts the gun to the cop's head again. "Your first mistake was coming here. Your second was coming alone."

The cop closes his eyes.

Travis holds the Ruger there, then takes it away, sticks it in his belt. He picks up another dish towel. Standing behind the cop, he wraps it around his right hand, makes a fist.

"I believe you, that you're looking for her," he says. "What happened, she promised you a share and then took off? I'll find her for both of us, how's that?"

The towel's tight across his knuckles. "Turn around. Go ahead. You can do it."

The cop pushes awkwardly away from the counter, turns to face him. Travis steps in, drives his fist into his face. The cop rebounds off the counter, falls loose and hard to the floor. He's out.

He unbuckles the cop's belt, pulls it free, uses it to tie his ankles. He'll be able to work them loose sooner or later, break a window, shout for help. Won't die here.

Everything he wants to take fits in his duffel bag. His

shoulder hurts now, a deep pain, as if something's broken loose inside.

The Silverado is a problem. The cop will have run the plate, what brought him here. He'll have to hide the truck somewhere, get it off the street. Another complication. He liked the Silverado, the power of it. And now he'll have to give it up, along with everything else in his life. Because of the woman.

He locks the door behind him, drops the cop's phone and keys into a storm drain. He gets into the Silverado, starts the engine, the duffel on the seat beside him.

On the run, he thinks. *Again.*

TWENTY-FIVE

IT'S SNOWING WHEN she gets off the train in Boston, takes a taxi to the hotel in Somerville. She locks the money in the room safe that's bolted low on the inner wall of the closet, black metal with a white keypad.

The room phone rings. When she answers, a man says, "Joanne Harper?"

"Joette."

"I'm calling for a friend. He got your message. He wants to see you."

"When?"

"I'll come to your hotel tomorrow at noon. Then, if everything's good, we'll take a ride."

"To where?"

"Tomorrow," he says, and the line disconnects.

Ten to noon and he's waiting for her downstairs, looking out of place standing there in the lobby. Late thirties, dark hair cut close, wearing an olive-drab flight jacket, hands in his pockets.

"Joette? Let's go. I'm out front."

It's a dark blue Lincoln with a tan roof, maybe ten years old but in good shape. When he pulls away from the curb, she says, "Where are we going?"

"Taking you to the man you came to see."

"Who are you?"

"Sean."

"Last name?"

"Sean's enough."

The streets are slushy with melted snow, the sky clear and bright. He glances at the rearview with each turn.

The diner is at the corner of a five-way intersection in the middle of a residential area. Weathered three-story houses, a few storefront businesses—what passed for a downtown in the days before zoning. The diner's a silver railroad car design. Neon above the door reads CLANCY'S.

The lot's almost full. He finds a spot, backs in, kills the engine.

"I don't know what you're doing here," he says. "Or what you want. But if I hear anything in there I don't like, I'm gonna walk you out, and then you're getting on the next train back to Jersey, you understand that?"

"Is he in there?"

"Remember what I said."

She follows him inside. Red leather booths, a mini-jukebox at each table. Behind the counter are desserts under glass. A handwritten sign taped to the register reads CASH ONLY. He nods to a booth in a far corner, where a white-haired man sits alone, reading a newspaper.

He looks up as she nears the booth, takes off his glasses. He's wearing a pale green work shirt, Carhartt pants, a tan zippered jacket. His shoulders are broad, his neck thick. His right ear is lumpy and deformed.

He folds the paper, puts it aside. In front of him is a half-eaten slice of key lime pie, black coffee in a ceramic mug. He gestures to the seat opposite.

"Joette," he says. "I get that right?"

"You did."

The waitress brings a coffeepot. "Pie not doing it for you today, Danny?"

"It's good, Alma. Just taking my time." To Joette, he says, "Something to eat?"

"Just coffee." Alma points to the upside-down mug on the table. Joette turns it over.

"Be careful, hon," Alma says as she pours. "He may look old and harmless, but watch out." She winks at Danny, tops off his mug and goes away.

"You look like your mother," he says.

"Do I?" She warms her hands around the mug.

"You do. Your eyes, your cheekbones. But now I'm afraid to ask."

"She had a stroke two years ago. She's been in a nursing home since."

"I'm sorry to hear that. Your father?"

"He died when I was a kid."

"How old were you?"

"Thirteen."

"That's tough. His name was Joseph, right?"

"It was."

"And you're Joette. They were expecting a boy?"

"Maybe."

"Harper's your married name?"

"It is."

"But you're not wearing a ring."

"My husband passed."

He picks up his mug. His fingers are blunt and thick, the knuckles scarred. "You've come a long way."

"Wasn't sure I'd be able to find you. I got a number from Information, a listing in Somerville, but the woman who answered said there was no one there named O'Dwyer. She gave me another number, turned out to be a liquor store."

"Sorry for the runaround. It's the neighborhood. They can be a little protective."

"I talked to someone there said he was the owner. Claimed he didn't know you either. I decided to take the leap, told him I was coming up here, when I'd arrive, where I'd be staying. Hoped the message would get to you."

"That was brave, come all this way, not knowing what you were going to find."

"I needed to get out of New Jersey for a while too. That was part of it. And I brought these."

She takes the packet of letters—bound with the faded red ribbon—from an inside pocket, sets them on the table. "I found them when I was emptying out her house."

He puts the glasses back on, picks up the envelopes, looks at the faint handwritten address on the top one. "Did you read them?"

"Some."

"They're from before she met your father."

"I know."

"Hard to believe she held on to them all these years."

"They must have been important to her," she says. "There may have been more, but these seven were all I found. There are two there that she wrote that came back undelivered and unopened."

"I moved around a lot in those days. I wasn't always easy to reach." He sets the packet down, takes off his glasses.

"She would talk about you sometimes. We saw something about you on TV once. Danny Boy O'Dwyer. I knew who you were. She said you'd grown up together."

"We did, a few blocks from here. That neighborhood's a lot different now. Nicer. I can hardly recognize it. Back then, it wasn't much to look at. But tight-knit, you know?"

"That's what she always said."

"The Conlons practically ruled the Hill. Your grandfather, Jimmy, was a serious man. Everybody was scared of him. Me too. I was taking a chance, going around with her."

"I never knew him. But I heard stories."

"I'm lucky that he liked me. Still, he told me if I ever did anything to hurt her, he'd put me at the bottom of the Charles. I believed him."

"She always wondered how things would have worked out if she'd stayed here. Whether it would have made any difference. If things might have gone a different way for you."

He shakes his head. "She was right to leave. And I was a hardhead back then. You couldn't tell me anything."

"You're not wearing a ring either. Are you married?"

"I was, forty-five years. My Grace is gone ten years ago this month."

"You have children?"

"She couldn't. We talked about adopting, back when we were first married. But I wasn't the best parental material as far as the agencies were concerned. Can't blame them."

"No other family?"

"I had a younger brother, Denny."

"Danny and Denny."

"A good kid. He made some of the same mistakes I did. I got away with most of them. I was lucky. He wasn't."

"He's dead?"

"He is. But you didn't come all the way up here to listen to an old man ramble."

"You weren't rambling. I asked."

"What about you? Kids?"

"No."

"Brothers, sisters?"

She shakes her head.

"So you're alone."

She looks back at the counter. Sean is on the last stool, drinking coffee, half turned to watch them.

"Speaking of protective," she says.

"My sister Nora's boy. He looks after me now. My age, I appreciate the company."

He sips coffee, sets the mug down. "Tell me about your father."

"What about him?"

"Was he a good man?"

"As far as it goes."

"What does that mean?"

"He had his issues. Like we all do."

"Many times I wondered how Irene was doing. If she was happy. If she had kids. Years I wondered that. And here you are."

"Here I am."

"With some fifty-year-old letters, and a problem you still haven't told me about."

"I need advice. And maybe more than that."

He sits back, watching her.

"My doctor says I'm supposed to get some exercise every day," he says. "Take a walk with me."

TWENTY-SIX

THE RIVER IS calm. No breeze at all. Ducks float along, undisturbed by the traffic on the bridge above. Boston in the distance, buildings gleaming in the afternoon sun.

Beside her, Danny rests his elbows on the railing, looking out at the water. She told him most of it on the walk here, Sean following them in the car. Now he watches them from the parking lot, leaning on the Lincoln's fender, hands in his pockets again.

"How much money are we talking about?" Danny says.

"A lot."

"And you took a shot at him too. He couldn't have been happy about that. Not that he didn't deserve it, from what you told me."

"I don't think I hurt him much."

"What was your plan if you'd killed him? Come up here, hide out?"

"I'm not sure. Part of me didn't think I'd be able to go ahead with it anyway."

"Good that you didn't. Killing a man, for whatever reason, that's a burden you carry a long time. It changes everything."

He rubs his chest.

"Are you all right?" she says.

"Bypass surgery last spring, second time. Takes it out of me to walk sometimes, but it's worse not to."

A seagull splashes into the water, then flies off. The ducks fan out, pedaling away from the ripples.

"If this guy was connected, I might be able to reach out," he says. "Somebody always knows somebody knows somebody else. At least that's the way it used to be. But from what you're saying, he sounds like a lone wolf."

"I'm worried what he might do to people around me. People he can get to."

"Like who?"

"He knows about the nursing home."

He looks at her. "How?"

"I'm not sure. But it's my fault. I've put others in danger as well."

"Any beef he has is between you and him. He shouldn't be threatening others. That's not a reasonable man. So maybe you can't reason with him after all."

"I could give him back the money."

"After all that? He'll kill you anyway, just to make his point. Maybe hurt somebody else near you beforehand, same reason."

"What should I do?"

He leans back against the railing, scratches an elbow. "Not

a lot of choices I see. One is, you go to the police, tell them everything."

"I'm not an innocent in all this. I could go to prison."

"Probably not. But you never know. You can't trust prosecutors, even if you cut a deal. I learned that the hard way. The other option you might be thinking of, though, the one you already tried, that's not something I can help you with."

"I'm not asking you to do anything."

A church bell rings the hour.

"You bring the money with you?"

"Some of it."

"That was risky, carrying it all the way up here."

"I didn't know what else to do with it."

She looks at Sean. He takes a pack of cigarettes from his jacket pocket, lights one, blows out smoke.

"He doesn't trust me," she says.

"He worries too much. I told him nobody cares about me anymore. I'm just a memory of the bad old days on the Hill. Soon everything I knew here will be gone, me with it. You ever been up here before? To the neighborhood?"

"No."

"Selective memory can get people confused, especially people my age. They talk about the old days, forget what it was really like. My old man was a longshoreman, took a fall from a container at the Commonwealth Pier. Broke his back. No disability back then. Out of work, out of luck. So I did what I had to do to put food on our table."

"That must have been tough."

"What I'm saying is, where you're from, it shapes you. Mass, New Jersey, wherever. Your life is what you see around you. Your values, choices, people you look up to. They all come out of that place. Your mother got away from all that. More importantly, she got away from *me*."

"It was still her home. She used to talk about it. About you."

"I did what I did. But when you're nineteen, twenty, you don't think about the future, who you might be hurting. You only think about yourself."

"She loved you. I know that."

"She used to write me when I was inside, that first time. After a while, I stopped reading the letters. Sent them back. Didn't even open them."

"Why?"

"You go inside, you can't dwell on what you lost. You have to keep your head straight, day to day. Think too much about what you don't have anymore, you drive yourself crazy."

"Do you want the letters?"

"Nah. The guy that wrote those, he's been gone for a long time. You keep them, or burn them, toss them, whatever you want."

"I would never do that."

"Funny thing is, looking at you brings all that back." He sighs. "Lotta years gone. Blink of an eye."

He looks back at the water. "Let me think about this, make a couple calls. Whether they'll do any good, I don't know. Maybe we can chase this guy off. Let him know he's out of his depth, who he's dealing with."

"Thank you."

"I'll do what I can. No promises."

"Of course."

"I'm not so good with those anyway," he says. "Your mother probably told you that, too."

Back at the hotel, she calls Brianna from her cell.

"Jo, where are you? I was worried."

"Nothing to worry about. I just had to go away for a little while. I wanted to get you this number, in case you need to reach me."

"Thank you for the check. I'll pay you back as soon as I can."

"Is everything okay there?"

Remembering Travis Clay in her rearview, standing with a gun by the side of the road. *Where is he now?*

"Yes. We're at my mom's. We can stay as long as we need."

"Good."

"Cara was asking about you, where you were."

"Give her a hug for me."

"I will. You sure everything's all right?"

"Maybe it will be," she says. "Soon."

After she ends the call, she opens the room safe, takes out a pack of hundreds, puts it in a hotel envelope.

Dusk brings more snow. She turns out the lights, stands at the window, watching it swirl in the streetlights below. The letters are on the dresser.

Mom, if you only knew where I am, who I saw.

The room phone trills.

"Our friend wants to meet," Sean says. "He's been thinking about your situation, has some ideas."

"When? Where?"

"Tonight. Your hotel. Nine o' clock. We'll come up."

"What does he think?"

"I'll let him tell you that," he says.

TWENTY-SEVEN

CAN SOLVE your problem," Danny says.

They're sitting in her room, Sean in a chair near the door, watching them.

"I talked to some people," Danny says. "I'm confident I can get this guy off your back."

"That was quick," she says.

"I still have a friend or two owes me a favor. But something like this, it costs."

"I expected that." She goes to the desk, opens a drawer and takes out the envelope, hands it to him.

"What's this?" he says.

"Ten thousand."

He looks at Sean, then back at her. "That's very generous." He tosses it on the bed.

"Not enough?" she says.

"Kid, I don't think you understand."

"What are you doing here?" Sean says. "Who sent you?"

"No one sent me."

"You wearing a wire?" He gets up.

"Don't touch me." Heat in her face, a swell of fear.

"Sean, let me handle this," Danny says. "Jo, this mess you got yourself into, you think your life's in danger, or you wouldn't be here. So we're not talking about any ten thousand, are we? Where it came from, what it was for, I'm guessing there was at least a hundred to start with."

She cuts a glance toward the door, Sean standing there, blocking it.

"I can deal with this for you," Danny says. "Take care of it like it never happened."

"And in return?"

"You're in way over your head here. You need to understand I'm doing you a favor. That money will only bring you more grief. Maybe we can make a deal, let you keep a little."

"That's what he said."

"Who?"

"The man I took it from."

He frowns. "I'd hate to see you get hurt. On your own, this only ends one way. You keep running, hope he doesn't find you. But from what you told me about this guy, he will."

"So you're going to help me?"

"Jo, I'm your best way out. I can settle this thing."

"In exchange for the money."

"Did you think you were going to be able to keep it?"

Sean gets up, slides open the closet door, flicks on the interior light. "There's a safe in here."

"That where you put it?" Danny says.

She doesn't answer. She's frozen.

"This is a good deal," Danny says. "You hand over the money—whatever you've got here—and your worries are over."

"A good deal," she says.

"Best you're gonna get. In your heart, you know I'm right."

"And if I say no?"

"Neither of us wants that."

She nods. "I was just wondering."

"About what?"

"What my mother would say if she was here."

His face hardens. "Let's not mix things up here. We had our talk about the old days. What's past is past. You brought those letters because you wanted something from me. Now I'm telling you what it'll cost."

"I need some time to think."

"What's there to think about?" Sean says. "Listen to the man. You don't have a choice."

"Or you'll kill me?"

"Don't talk foolish," Danny says. "But wanting time to think, that doesn't work either, and you know why. First chance you get, you're out of town, and we're left holding the bag. No. The way it has to go, when we walk out that door, it's settled."

"Open the safe," Sean says.

"Look at it as a weight off your shoulders," Danny says. "Maybe all I have to do is have a conversation with this guy, discourage him. He gets the message, and you're in the clear."

"He won't give up. He hasn't so far."

"Then we do what has to be done. Either way, you're free. Now, I'm guessing Sean's right, the money's in the safe. You told me you brought it here, and you haven't had time to do anything with it. So let's have a look at what's in there, come to an agreement."

"And you'll settle for that?"

"We'll talk about it. Jo, you don't know what you're into here. You ever want to go back to a normal life, this is what you have to do."

"Normal," she says.

"That's right."

She turns to Sean. His right hand's in his coat pocket.

"You have a gun in there?" she says. "Make a lot of noise, wouldn't it? Shoot me in a hotel room?"

"I don't need a gun." His hand comes out of the pocket.

"Everybody settle down, all right?" Danny says. "I think Jo knows what the situation is."

"I do," she says, and suddenly the fear is gone. It all feels inevitable now, like she's watching it, what's going to happen.

"If you have a gun, go ahead and shoot me," she says. "Best ending to this for me anyway, isn't it?"

"Nobody's shooting anybody," Danny says. "Jo, be reasonable."

Sean takes a step closer.

"Come on, Jo," Danny says. "Don't make us the bad guys."

"It's not all there. I left some in banks back home."

"Let's take a look," Danny says. "We can work this out."

She's surprised how calm she feels. She slides the closet door wider, kneels in front of the safe. Sean's shadow falls across her.

"You're in my light," she says. He steps to the side.

She taps in the combination, and the green light blinks. She pulls open the door. He can see the packs of banded money.

"There we go," he says.

She reaches past the money, feels the .25 on the shelf there, draws it out, and aims it at his groin. "Leave."

He takes a step back. "Get the fuck out of here with that."

"Put that down, Jo," Danny says. "Are you crazy?"

She stands, her legs tingling, numb. She thumbs off the safety, backs up, bumps against the desk.

"We don't want a scene here," Danny says. "Don't make this worse."

"What is that, a twenty-five?" Sean says. "You ever fire that thing? You shoot me with that, I might not even feel it."

"You'll feel it. Don't come any closer."

Danny puts out his hand. "Give me that before somebody gets hurt."

Sean lunges. She throws herself back, hits the desk, and then she's falling, taking the chair down with her. She squeezes the trigger, and the gun goes off with a crack.

Sean leaps back. She's missed. Then he reaches down, grips his right leg. There's a hole in his jeans, halfway down the inside of his calf.

"Bitch, you shot me."

She gets up, using the desk for support, the gun still pointed at him.

"Now look what you did," Danny says. "Enough of this."

She swings the gun toward him. He raises his hands, backs away. Sean sits down in the chair. He slides up his jeans leg, exposes a small hole in the fleshy part of his calf, blood streaming slowly out.

"I'm bleeding."

She backs up to keep both of them in front of her.

"Use your belt," Danny says.

Sean looks at him.

"On your leg."

He unbuckles the belt. It's thin, black leather with a silver buckle. He pulls it free of the loops, wraps it around his leg just above the hole and threads the belt through the buckle.

"On the outside," Danny says. "You gonna walk down the hall like that?"

He undoes the belt, eases the jeans leg down, then tightens it again, grimaces.

"There you go," Danny says.

Danny looks at her, lowers his hands, something like a smile on his face. "You made your point."

He reaches for the envelope.

"No," she says. "It's too late." Surprised to hear herself saying the words. "Leave it."

"Now, that's not right."

"It was all a lie, wasn't it? About making phone calls, talking to people?"

"No. I can still make that happen."

"Get out."

"Lady, you fucked up," Sean says. His face is shiny with sweat.

She points the gun at him. "Wouldn't be the first time. Out."

"Seems I misjudged you," Danny says.

"You did." Her arm is tired now. The gun wavers.

To Sean, he says, "Can you walk?"

"I think so."

"I know a doctor we can call, get you fixed up. I'll drive. Try not to bleed in the car."

"What about her?"

"Just leave," she says.

At the door, Danny turns back to her.

"You got heart, kid," he says. "Keep the money. You earned it."

When they're gone, she packs quickly. The envelope and the money from the safe go back into her suitcase.

She takes the gun, slides out the clip. It's empty. The bullet in the chamber is the only one left.

Outside the hotel, the snow's coming down harder. No sign of the Lincoln. A taxi pulls up to the entrance, its wipers thumping. She gets in back, drags the suitcase in with her. "South Station."

"You want to put that in the trunk?" the driver says.

"No. I'll keep it with me."

As they pull away, she looks back at the hotel. No one's following them.

Her left hand begins to shake. She opens and closes her fist until it stops.

He was right. You can keep running, but to where? Sooner or later, you'll have to go back.

An hour later, she's on a train heading south. The car's dim. She looks out at the driving snow, listens to the wheels.

They pass a row of homes, windows full of light. She imagines the people inside, children, families, warm and safe. Then it's dark again, and all she can see is her own reflection. She touches the coolness of the glass.

TWENTY-EIGHT

TWO A.M. AND Travis is parked in the lot of the strip club, alone in the Lexus. He left the Silverado in the garage at Cosmo's town house in Manalapan, locked and tarped. He'll need new wheels before long. The Lexus is too noticeable, easy to remember. No good for what he has planned.

The bar is a squat concrete building with blacked-out windows, a sign that reads HI-STEPPERS GENTLEMAN'S CLUB. It's closing time, only a few cars left in the lot. As he watches, burly men in STAFF T-shirts walk girls to their cars.

His shoulder itches, burns. Infection setting in. He'll have to change the dressing again soon.

A Denali with darkened windows pulls up to the entrance. He remembers it from the motel. The club door opens, and Brianna comes out carrying a shoulder bag, gets in the passenger side. She told him about the club when he met her, and he took the chance coming here.

He follows the Denali out of the lot. Traffic is sparse, so it's easy to keep it in sight. Fifteen minutes later, it turns into the entrance of a condo complex. He follows but stays back, switches off his headlights. The Denali's brake lights flare as it pulls into a driveway, noses up to a garage door. There's a light in the house's front window.

He drives on. The street dead-ends two blocks later in a circular cul-de-sac. He turns around, pulls to the curb, watches them get out of the Denali. The driver is young and skinny, wearing a sideways baseball cap. Brianna unlocks the front door, and they go in. A few minutes later, the man comes out alone, gets in the Denali and drives away. The house light goes off.

He gives it another half hour, then gets out of the Lexus, walks to the house, staying in the shadows between the light poles.

The house is quiet. He slips into the side yard, takes out his penlight, shines it through the garage window. There's a compact minivan inside. He tracks the narrow beam across the floor. Leaning against the rear wall is what he was looking for. The pink bicycle.

He douses the light and walks back to the Lexus.

———

When he gets back to Cosmo's, there's an empty pint bottle of vodka in the kitchen trash bin. The smell of pot smoke lingers in the air.

Cosmo is snoring loudly. His bedroom door is ajar, the overhead light still on. He's lying atop the covers facedown, fully dressed.

There's a prescription pill bottle on the nightstand. Travis picks it up, reads the label. Xanax. Cosmo self-medicating his stress.

He sets the bottle back down, turns off the light, closes the door behind him.

In the bathroom, he pulls off his T-shirt, gingerly peels away the gauze from his shoulder. It's black with dried blood, patches of yellow pus that weren't there before. The skin around the wound is red and warm. He dabs at it with a wet washcloth, then tapes on more gauze.

He feels dizzy then, has to sit on the rim of the tub until it passes. He takes two Tylenol from the medicine cabinet, washes them down with tap water. He'll need something stronger soon.

Awake in the guest bedroom, he looks up at the ceiling, working it out in his head, what he'll do tomorrow, how to turn all this around. The pain in his shoulder is a rhythmic pulse, fading as he drifts into sleep.

———

The next afternoon, Cosmo drives him to the Middletown commuter lot. Cosmo is sallow and sick. Before they left the town house, Travis could hear him throwing up behind the bathroom door.

"You keeping it together?" Travis says as they pull into the lot. "You don't look too good."

"I'll be all right. Just a bad night."

"You need to take it easy with the drinking. I need you sharp."

"I just got to thinking about all that's going on. Maybe it's time we cut our losses."

"How's that?"

"We still have the fifty in the safe. We can split that, lay low, let some of this shit blow over."

"Twenty-five each? How long will that last? Besides, there's a principle involved."

"What principle?"

Travis doesn't answer.

"Is it worth it," Cosmo says, "keep chasing that money?"

"It'll be over soon."

"Will it? Everything you told me, doesn't seem like that woman's going to give it up."

"She will this time," Travis says. "I have a plan."

He gets out of the Lexus, waits for Cosmo to drive away, then walks the rows of cars until he finds one he knows he can hot-wire easily, a four-door Saturn. The rear passenger door is unlocked. A good sign, his luck coming back around.

He uses the tactical knife to pry off part of the steering column, then strips and braids wires until the engine starts.

He gets on the Parkway and heads south, then east toward the ocean, following the coast roads. Past the Manasquan Inlet are the abandoned beach houses he remembered, four of them in a row, flooded out by the last hurricane, waiting to be torn down.

The southernmost house is farther away from the others, more battered. The windows and doors are covered with plywood. The gray paint's been stripped off the walls by years of wind-blown sand.

He parks across the road near a shuttered pavilion and bandshell. No one around. He crosses the sandy street, walks through the dune grass to the beach. The wind is coming hard off the ocean. Waves slam into the stone jetties, spray geysering high.

There's a deck in back of the last house, the redwood long faded, gaps in the rotted boards. Two sheets of plywood are nailed over a frame that once held a sliding glass door. One of them is loose. He pulls on it, nails squeaking, until it comes away. He leans it against the other sheet, shines the penlight inside. It's a small kitchen, stripped bare, sand on the floor.

Beyond the kitchen is a dark hall with two facing doors. The right one opens on a bedroom with a boarded window, a stained mattress on the floor. On the left, a bathroom with a narrow plastic shower stall and a sink bleeding rust.

At the end of the hall is the living room. Fast-food cartons on the floor, beer cans, a burned-out pack of matches and a bent spoon. There's a collapsed canvas folding chair on the floor near a small fireplace. Wind whistles through gaps in the plywood.

A calmness comes over him. He's been in constant motion, reacting rather than planning, forced to make decisions on the fly. He's felt it all getting away from him, the risks increasing. Now he can control the situation again, make things happen the way he wants, when he wants. Bring them all to him, and finish it here.

TWENTY-NINE

A NIGHTMARE WAKES her. Joette sits up with a start, slick with sweat, pushes the sheets away. She sits on the edge of the bed, head in her hands. She can't shake the dream. Troy calling to her out of blackness, a warning. But his voice was faint and far away, lost in the wind. She couldn't make out the words.

Stay with me. Don't leave me alone, she answered. But he was already gone.

She goes to the window, looks out at the morning. The hotel is in Tinton Falls, just off the Parkway. She got into New Jersey at 4 a.m., tired and wired, rented a car in Newark and drove south.

A shower makes her feel better, the bathroom filling with steam, the heat untangling her muscles. She tries Noah's cell, but after six rings it goes to voice mail. She leaves a message. An hour later, he still hasn't called back. Something's wrong.

She locks the money in the room safe, then drives to his house in Millstone Township. It's an old farmhouse set back from the road, with a gravel driveway. His truck is parked out front. She pulls her rental Ford in behind it.

She doesn't have to knock. Noah opens the door, looks out at her through the screen. He has a black eye, and there's a strip of surgical tape across the bridge of his nose.

Noah, what did you do?

"Jo," he says. "I thought that might be you."

"What happened?"

He slips the hook-and-eye latch, pushes the screen door open. She follows him into the kitchen. There's a gun holstered on his right hip.

"I'm glad to see you," he says. "Was wondering if I would."

"I called and left a message. You didn't call me back."

He opens the refrigerator. "Something to drink? Couple Bud Lights in here. I had some Blue Moons awhile back, but I guess I drank them."

"Tell me."

He takes out a bottle of water, opens it, turns to her. "I didn't call you back because I wasn't sure what to say."

"And now?"

"You'd disappeared. I hadn't heard from you, had no idea where you were, or what happened. So I went to see this Travis Clay."

"Christ, Noah, why?"

"Find out what he knew. Maybe scare him off."

"You shouldn't have gone there. There was no reason."

"I wanted to know what the deal was between you and him. I'm still not sure."

"There's no deal. Only what I already told you."

He could have been killed, and that would have been on you. And now you're lying to him again.

"You went there alone?" she says.

"I didn't want anyone else involved, until I knew what was going on, where you figured in."

"I'm not your responsibility, Noah. I've never asked you to solve my problems."

"I was worried."

"He hurt you."

"Not so bad. Nose got the worst of it. Some sore ribs, nothing else. I'm tougher than I look."

"Where is he now?"

He sips water. "I don't know."

"Is there a warrant out on him?"

"Not yet. I haven't told anyone about this. I've been calling in sick."

"Why?"

"Story gets a little complicated, doesn't it? What I was doing there, where you fit in. Not easy to explain. And he said some things to me I didn't understand. Like he was assuming I knew more than I did."

He's different now. He doesn't trust you anymore.

"I also ran a check on the driver of the car that wrecked outside the motel—Nash. Don't know why it took me so long. Never occurred to me before, I guess."

"And?"

"He and Clay were in prison at the same time a few years back. Rahway. Coincidence, isn't it? I mean, not impossible, a couple of lowlifes like that, in and out of jail. But maybe there's a connection there."

"What kind of connection?"

"That's what I've been trying to figure out," he says. "Like maybe Clay is the one shot this Nash guy. Then he came to the motel to find out what you knew, what you saw. But that doesn't make any sense, him exposing himself like that. So it had to be something else brought him there."

"And you think I'm involved?"

"I don't know what to think. You walk off your job. Your trailer gets torched. You're mixed up—somehow—with some scumbag ex-con. Hard not to think something's going on. I just don't know what it is."

"I'm sorry I asked you to run that plate. I shouldn't have. I didn't want any of this to come back on you."

"Talk to me now, Jo, while I can still help. Before it's out of my hands."

"No one else knows about this?"

"Not yet, but it'll only take a phone call."

"Would you do that?"

"If I have to."

"Don't. Please."

"Jo, if you're into something, if there's trouble ahead, you need to get out in front of it. I know people in the prosecutor's office we can talk to. That's the way these things work when there's others involved—first deal, best deal. Longer you wait, the worse your chances are."

There it is again. The choice. You can still tell him everything. Take what's coming.

"What about it?" he says. "I can get on the phone right now."

"I'm sorry you got hurt, Noah. That was the last thing I wanted."

"If you don't listen to me, I can't guarantee what happens next. This isn't a game."

"I never thought it was."

"And that's all you've got to say?"

"I'm not keeping anything from you. You know everything that I do."

"I don't think I believe that. I'm trying to do the right
thing here, Jo. You're not making it easy."

"It never is," she says.

———————

As she backs out of the driveway, she sees him behind the
screen, looking out at her. Then he closes the door.

THIRTY

HE FOLLOWS THE Denali home from the strip club again, parks the Saturn in the darkness of the cul-de-sac, unbraids wires to kill the engine.

Once the woman and the driver are in the house, he gets out, walks quickly up the street. By the garage door, he pulls on the ski mask he's brought, flexes his gloves to loosen them.

When the driver comes back out, Travis steps in behind him, puts the Ruger in his back. "Right there's good. Don't yell. Don't run."

The driver raises his hands. "If you want the wheels, man, take 'em."

"You have a key to the house?"

"This one? No."

"Knock on the door. I'll be right behind you. When it

opens, you're going in. Try to make a move, I'll kill you and whoever's on the other side." He prods him with the gun. "Go."

The driver goes to the door, knocks tentatively.

"Louder," Travis says. He stays behind him to his right, out of sight.

The door opens. Brianna says, "Hey, babe, you forget something?"

Travis pushes him forward into her. She stumbles back, and he shows her the gun. "Don't scream."

They're in a half-lit living room. The little girl is asleep on a couch, a blanket pulled up around her.

Travis eases the door closed behind him. "Anybody else in the house?"

"No," Brianna says. "Don't hurt us."

"Do what I say, and I won't. Do anything else, and I'll kill all of you. The girl, too."

Do they recognize his voice, remember him from the day he fixed the bike?

"Get the girl," he says. "We're going to take a ride. Bring a blanket, whatever you need for her."

"I'm not leaving here," Brianna says. There's fear in her eyes, but anger, too. He'll have to watch her.

He touches the gun muzzle to the side of the driver's head. "You ready to watch what happens next?"

"Why are you doing this?"

"You know why."

There's a tremor in the driver's voice. "Bree, let's do what he says."

"What's your name?" Travis says.

"Keith."

"Keith, here's where we find out how much your girlfriend loves you."

"Don't," she says. "Just take me."

"I need the three of you. Keith will drive. I'll show you where we're going." He lowers the gun. "You ride in front with the girl. If she wakes up, keep her calm. Do what I tell you, and you'll all be back here before dawn."

"Where are you taking us?" Brianna says.

"Bring your phone."

"Why?"

"You want to get out from under this—all of you—you need to make a call. Or however many it takes until you reach her. If you can't, then things are gonna end bad. You know who I'm talking about."

"I told you," Keith says. "I told you she'd get us in trouble."

"You should have listened to him," Travis says. "He was right."

THIRTY-ONE

THEY PARK ON the street near the beach house. Blowing sand clicks against the Denali.

"I want to go home," Cara says. "I'm cold." She woke up halfway through the twenty-minute ride.

"We will, angel, soon," Brianna says.

"Give me your cell phones," Travis says.

He pockets them, touches the woman's shoulder and points to the house. "Take the girl, go around to the back. It's open. Go inside and wait for me."

"What about me?" Keith says. His hands are tight on the wheel.

"I need you here."

"I'm not going without him," she says.

"He'll be fine. No one gets hurt if you listen, remember?"

He hands her the penlight. "Bring this. You'll need it."

"No."

"You want to force the issue? Right here? Make me do something I don't want to?"

She takes the penlight from him, opens the door. Hoisting the girl up, she tightens the blanket around her. They start toward the house, heads down against the wind. He watches the penlight beam move through the dune grass, then disappear.

He puts a hand on Keith's shoulder, feels the tension there. "Relax. You're doing fine. Pull into that pavilion across the street, park behind the bandstand, close as you can get. Then cut the lights and engine."

"Why?"

"Just do it. You'll be okay. This isn't about you."

Keith U-turns in the street, pulls into the pavilion lot and around to the back of the bandshell. He turns off the engine and lights, looks at Travis in the rearview.

"Now it's just the two of us, you can tell me," Travis says. "Where is she?"

"I don't know. Something happened, I'm not sure what. She took off."

"When did you see her last?"

"A few days ago, in Atlantic City. She wanted to meet. She gave me some money, for Brianna."

"My money," Travis says.

"I don't know where it came from."

"I'm telling you where it came from. Have either of you seen her since?"

He shakes his head.

"Have they talked?"

"On the phone, yeah."

"She's still in Jersey?"

"As far as I know."

"You don't know much."

Better to kill him now, Travis thinks. Take him out of play. But then he'd have to kill the woman and the girl, too.

He gets out on the driver's side, gun in hand, leaves the door open. "Come out, slow. Take off on me and you won't get three feet. I'll put a bullet in your spine, leave you on the ground."

Keith opens his door, slides out. Travis takes the cap from his head, tosses it into the backseat. "Get in."

When he hesitates, Travis whips the butt of the gun into his left temple. It drops him to his knees. Just enough pain to keep him from doing something stupid.

"Up."

Travis sets the gun on the roof, takes zip ties from his pocket. He binds Keith's hands behind him, pushes him facedown onto the rear seat. "Get on in there." He ties his ankles.

"I could gag you to keep you quiet," he says. "Run the risk you'll choke to death. Do I need to do that?"

"No."

"Because if I hear you out here, calling for help, making noise, I'm going to come back and shoot you in the head. There's nobody around anyway, so save your breath. Just lay there and be quiet."

He shuts the doors, takes the Ruger from the roof. The pain in his shoulder is back, extends down his arm. He's sweating despite the cold.

Sand stings his face as he crosses the road. He passes through the waving dune grass, starts toward the house, puts away the gun. He doesn't want to scare the woman and the girl any more than he has. He needs them under control, doing what he says, not panicked.

They're huddled in the living room, sitting with their

backs to the wall. He found two short candles in the kitchen earlier. Now he sets them on the mantelpiece, lights them with a plastic lighter. Their glow dances on the walls.

"Where is he?" the woman says.

"Across the street, waiting for you. I just needed him out of the way for a while."

"Don't hurt my mom," the girl says.

"I won't. If she does what I say."

"I'm not scared of you, whoever you are. Or your gun."

He takes the two cell phones from his jacket pocket, puts them on the floor in front of the woman.

"What do you want?" she says.

"Call her."

"Who?"

"Play it that way, it'll be a long night. I figure at least one of these has her new number. No way she takes off, doesn't leave you a way to get in touch with her."

"I don't know where she is. She could be anywhere."

"Then we'll just have to wait for her, won't we? However long it takes."

He pushes the phones toward her. "Make that call."

The phone jolts Joette out of sleep. It's vibrating on the nightstand, light blinking. She reaches for it, sees the time—Brianna's number. Something bad.

She opens the line. "Bree?"

Silence, then Travis Clay's voice. "I wake you?"

"Where did you get that phone?"

"Where do you think? Someone here wants to talk to you."

Brianna comes on the line. "Jo, he made me call. I'm sorry."

"Is Cara with you? Are you all right?"

"Yes…"

He takes the phone away. "That's enough for now."

"Don't hurt them."

"You don't get to make demands anymore," he says. "All you get to do is to shut up and listen."

"I'm listening."

"What I'm going to tell you, I'll only say once. You screw it up, pull anything, complicate anything, and it's over. Then I call you back and make you listen to a sound that'll haunt you for the rest of your life."

THIRTY-TWO

JOETTE SHUTS OFF the car, looks at the beach house a block away. She can see faint light around the edges of boarded-over windows.

If you go in there, you'll die.

The money is in a sports bag in the trunk, a little less than $250,000. All that's left. She has to trust him, that he'll let Cara and Brianna go in exchange for the money. But she knows he won't leave her alive.

She takes the .25 from her vest pocket, unlocks the slide, checks the bullet in the chamber. Last one. If she can distract him with the money long enough, she might be able to bring out the gun, pull the trigger. She'll aim for his face.

This is where it ends. Where it's been headed all along.

Wind shakes the car. She calls Brianna's number. When Travis Clay answers, she says, "I'm here."

"Come around back. I'll be waiting for you."

She gets the bag from the trunk, slips the gun into her right rear jeans pocket, flat against her hip.

The wind is loud. The dune grass sways around her, seems to whisper as she moves through it.

She starts up the beach toward the house. A dark figure comes out onto the deck, wearing a ski mask, watching her. When she reaches the steps, he raises a gun, letting her know it's there.

"I should shoot you where you stand," he says. "All the trouble you caused."

She slips the bag off her shoulder. "Here it is."

"Bring it up."

He won't kill her until he has a look at the money, she thinks. He'll want to know how much she's brought.

"Go on in," he says. "And say hello."

She walks through into a dark kitchen. Candlelight flickers at the end of a hallway. She feels his gun at her back.

"Where are they?" she says.

"Door on the right. Go ahead, open it."

It's a bedroom. Brianna sits on a mattress in shadow, Cara asleep in her arms, her head on her mother's shoulder. A candle on the floor is burning low.

"I'm sorry, Jo," Brianna says.

"I'm the one who's sorry. Are you both all right?"

Brianna nods. Cara stirs but doesn't wake.

"Take off," he says to Brianna. "Your boyfriend's waiting for you. Keys are in the ignition."

"Did you hurt him?" Brianna says.

"Gave him a headache. That's all. Go, before I change my mind."

Cara wakes, rubs her eyes, looks up. "Jo, is that you?"

"It's me, kiddo. How are you doing?"

"Let's go," he says. "There'll be time to talk later."

Brianna gets up, holding Cara close. "I'll wait for you."

"No," Joette says. "You need to go home. I'll be okay." Wanting them far away from him.

"She's right," he says. "We're just going to talk some business."

Cara wraps her arms around her mother's neck.

"Go on," Joette says. "Please."

"I'll keep your phones," he says. "Just in case you're tempted to make a call, get someone else involved. That would be bad for everybody."

He moves aside to let them pass. When they're gone, Joette says, "Did you kill him?"

"No, he's there. Like I told her." He pokes her side with the gun. "Down the hall. Move."

In the living room, a candle flutters on the mantelpiece, throws shadows on the wall. Her feet brush against trash. He touches the cold muzzle to the nape of her neck.

This is where you'll die. In this room. This darkness.

Her back to him, she holds out the bag. "Your money."

"Glad to hear you call it that. If you'd realized that sooner, it would have been easier for all of us."

He takes the bag, sets it down. "Cell phone."

She hands it to him. He drops it on the bag. "Where's your car?"

"On the beach road. About a block away."

"Rental?"

"Yes."

"Give me the keys." He takes them from her hand.

An engine starts outside. The noise grows fainter, then there's only the wind.

"Don't get your hopes up," he says. "Even if they go for help, we'll be done before anyone gets here. And I'm thinking they won't try anyway. You're the one put them in danger to start with."

"I made a mistake."

"More than one."

"Whatever happens, leave them alone."

The gun comes away from her neck.

"If I do have to pay them a visit, it'll be no one's fault but yours. Don't think otherwise. Now turn around."

Her hand drifts closer to the .25 in her pocket. Off in the distance, something bangs in the wind.

She turns to face him, looks into those pale gray eyes behind the mask. He moves the gun to his left hand, flexes his right. His gloved fist is a blur.

THIRTY-THREE

WHEN SHE COMES to, she's on the floor, her face against cold wood. Shadows move on the wall. The left side of her face is swollen, and she can taste blood.

He's sitting on a canvas chair by the fireplace, counting money, the sports bag open at his feet, the candle beside it. No mask now.

Wind blows through the house, brings the smell of the ocean. Eyes half closed, she looks down the hallway to the kitchen, the deck beyond. Wonders if she has the strength to get up, run for it. The speed to make it outside before he shoots her in the back.

"Hey," he says. "Come on, wake up. I didn't hit you that hard. Not as hard as I wanted to. Felt good, though."

She keeps still, trying to buy time, clear her head.

"I was trying to figure out how much you held back," he

says. "But it doesn't matter at this point, does it? It's not about the money. Hasn't been for a while."

He gets up, kicks her leg. "Wake up. Look at me."

His fingers tangle in her hair. He twists and pulls up sharp, drags her to her knees. The pain makes her gasp. Her right hand goes to her back pocket. It's empty.

He holds up the .25. "Looking for this?"

She tries to pull away, and he twists her hair tighter. "Plenty of times you could have put a stop to this. But you couldn't help yourself, could you?"

He lets go and she falls back. He crouches in front of her.

"Only one round in here. Optimistic on your part, wasn't it? Now, did I take it out of the chamber, or not?"

He pushes the muzzle into the soft skin below her jaw, twists it there, angling upward. "One way to find out."

She closes her eyes. Wonders if she'll feel the bullet. If she'll even know.

"Not much fun, is it?" he says. "Having a gun pointed at you. Not much fun getting shot either."

The gun clicks.

She starts to shake.

"Guess I did," he says.

She opens her eyes. He takes the gun away. He's sitting back on his haunches, three feet from her, the side of his face lit by the guttering candle. His own gun's on top of the money bag, out of his reach.

No. You're not going to die. Not like this. Not here. Not now.

His jacket is open, and she can see the slight bulge beneath his shirt on his left shoulder. Bandages covering where she shot him.

There.

She twists her hips, pumps her right leg out, drives her heel into his shoulder. He falls back, and she swivels on the floor in the same movement, kicks at the candle with her left foot, sends it flying. The room goes dark.

Get out.

She's on her feet. He rolls into her, grabs at her legs. His hand closes tight on her right ankle, and she kicks at his face, feels it connect. His grip loosens, and then she's free, moving past him, running through the darkness toward the kitchen. The crack of his gun behind her, and a bullet whines past her ear. The next one will be in her back.

He fires again just as she reaches the deck. She hears the shot pass above her, leaps off the steps into the hard sand. It drives the breath out of her. She pushes against the ground, gets her legs under her, runs. Panic is a siren in her head.

Another crack, louder than the wind. Sand kicks up to her right. The dune grass is ahead. *You can lose him there.*

She cuts to the left, heading for the waving shadows, hears his feet on the sand behind her. He's panting as he runs.

She's almost at the dune grass when he catches her. He grips her hair, drags her off-balance, kicks her leg out from under her. She lands on her back, and then he's straddling her, his left hand around her throat, leaning his weight into her. She can't get air. She pulls at his hand, tries to pry his fingers loose.

"Fucking stop fighting me." He pushes the warm muzzle into her face, just below her cheekbone. His finger is on the trigger.

No.

She grabs his wrist with both hands, shoves the gun away. His weight comes forward, and the barrel slides into the sand just as he fires. Sand explodes, showers down around them. She tries to hold on to his wrist, but he jerks it free, jams the gun into her side, twisting it up under her rib cage. She waits for the ripping heat of the bullet. Hears the gun snap and click.

The Ruger's slide locks back half open, the trigger seizes. In that instant, he knows what's happened. The vacuum of the recoil sucked sand into the barrel, jammed the mechanism.

He raises the gun high, the butt reversed. He'll finish it like this. Hammer away at her face, keep hitting her until all the bones are broken and she's drowning in her own blood.

She sees the gun go up, raises her left hand to ward it off, punches at his shoulder with her right. She hears his sharp intake of breath, knows it hurt him. Her fingers close on the dressing through his shirt, and she pushes her thumb into it, digging, twisting. He jerks away from her, shifts his balance, and that's all she needs. She swings her hips to the side, squirms out from beneath him, shoves him away. He falls back in the sand, and then she's on her feet again, running.

She crashes through the dune grass, trips on something, sprawls into the sand. She reaches down and feels a crooked piece of driftwood half buried there, three feet long and hard as stone.

He's almost on her. She grips the driftwood, swings wild with it, hits him in the left knee. He grunts in pain, and she rolls away from him as he falls. Then she's standing over him, holding the driftwood in both hands.

He looks up at her, and she brings the driftwood down

across the side of his head, feels the impact. The blow knocks him sideways in the sand, his legs twisted under him.

She raises the driftwood high again. He's motionless at her feet.

Hit him again.

But she can't do it, not like this. The driftwood seems to grow heavier. She drops it, takes two dizzy steps back and sits down in the sand, gasping for breath. The wind howls around her.

THIRTY-FOUR

*Y*OU CAN'T STAY HERE.

She stands, her ankle numb from her fall. He hasn't moved. A line of blood is creeping out of his hairline.

She gets her car keys from his jacket pocket. Then she walks grids until she finds the gun, a darker shape against the sand. She takes it out onto the jetty, stepping carefully on the slippery rocks, throws it as far as she can out into the water.

She's dizzy as she limps back to the house. In the dark living room, her foot hits something that clatters away. She reaches down, feels for it. It's a penlight. She switches it on, and the beam shows her the trash-strewn floor, the .25, the cell phones. The bag with the money.

Her hands shake as she drives. A few blocks from the beach house, her vision begins to blur. There's a stab of pain behind her left eye, and for a moment she thinks she's going to pass out.

Something moves in front of her headlights. She hammers the brake, jerks the wheel to the right. The Ford's front tire hits the curb with a jolt, climbs it, then rolls back down. There's nothing in the road.

You can't drive. You'll kill yourself or someone else.

She turns down a side street of dark summer homes, vacant for the season. She pulls into an empty driveway, shuts off the engine and lights, rests her head on the steering wheel.

Don't fall asleep. Don't...

A gust of wind moves the car. She opens her eyes, doesn't know how much time has passed. Nausea swells up, and she wants to vomit, holds it back.

She takes the sports bag from the passenger seat, gets out. She'll walk until she finds someplace with people, lights.

Back on the beach road, sand and wind sting her face. Her vision slips out of focus again. The ground tilts under her, and she falls onto her side.

Get up.

She pushes the ground away, counts her steps. At fifteen, she falls again.

She looks out at the dark ocean, hears Troy's voice inside the wind. *Get up. Walk.*

"Don't leave me, baby," she says. "Don't leave me alone again."

Get up.

Far down the beach road, headlights are coming slow. They stop, and she's blinded by their glare.

The driver's door opens and Brianna gets out, runs toward her.

Joette tries to smile, but it hurts too much.

———————

Sand blows in the headlights as they drive.

"You came back," Joette says.

"I couldn't leave you there."

"Where's Cara?"

"With Keith. She's safe. As soon as I got them inside, I turned around and headed back. I was afraid he'd killed you."

"You were taking a chance, doing that."

"Your face."

She touches her jaw, feels a flash of pain.

"Is he coming after us?" Brianna says.

"No."

"Is he dead?"

She doesn't answer.

———————

Keith's place is a garden apartment in Brick Township. He jumps up from the couch when the door opens.

"Where's Cara?" Brianna says.

"In my room," he says. "Sleeping."

Joette brings in the sports bag. Her ankle hurts with each step.

"We should get you to a hospital," Brianna says. "And maybe it's time to call the police."

"No." The room begins to spin slowly. She puts a hand on the back of a chair. "You have another bed here?"

"In the back," he says. "It's made, but there's only a mattress, no box spring."

"I don't care."

She carries the bag down the hall, stops at a half-open door. Cara is sleeping on the bed inside. The hall light falls across her face, her pale blond hair. Joette watches her breathe, then quietly closes the door.

There are no curtains in the back room. Dawn is a faint glow outside the window.

Her head aches, but her vision is clear. She shuts the door, sets the bag against it, lies facedown on the mattress, and is instantly asleep.

THIRTY-FIVE

THE WIND WAKES him. He's lying in the dune grass, sand under him, his clothes damp and cold. He can hear the waves.

He touches the left side of his head, the hair stiff with blood there, feels the three-inch-long furrow. The driftwood glanced off his head at an angle, her aim uncertain in the darkness. Hard enough to knock him out, but not to kill him.

He crawls, kneels, then pushes himself to his feet, finds his balance. His shoulder is on fire, the dressing there loose.

He pats his jacket pocket. Her keys are gone. He looks around but can't find the Ruger.

His left knee throbs, but he can walk. The house is empty. The bag with the money is gone, along with her gun and the cell phones.

He's shaky, ready to fall again. He has to get out of here, keep moving, get back to Cosmo's.

His knee aches as he walks the beach road. The sky over the ocean is growing lighter. The wind's begun to slacken. After a block, he hears an engine, turns to see a blue van coming up behind him.

He steps into the road, waves. The van slows to a stop. The paint is sun-faded, the panels pitted with rust. The driver is young and bearded, wearing coveralls. He puts the window down as Travis comes up to him. "Man, what happened to you?"

"I've been in an accident. Can you take me to a hospital?"

"An accident? Where?"

Travis gestures vaguely behind him. "Back there somewhere. I'm hurt bad."

"You need to call 911."

"No police."

"Why? You been drinking?"

"Yeah. I can't afford another DWI." He moves closer to the door, gauging angles, distance.

"Anybody else hurt?"

"No."

"I still think you need to—"

Travis steps up on the running board, punches him in the temple, snaps his head to the side. He slumps forward against the shoulder belt, and Travis leans in and hits him again in the same place. The driver's foot slips off the brake, and the van begins to move forward. Travis reaches in and shuts off the ignition. The van rolls to a stop.

No traffic, the nearby houses dark. He opens the door, undoes the driver's shoulder harness and drags him out. A cell phone is clipped to his belt. Travis leaves him in the weeds on the side of the road, takes the phone.

He climbs into the van, starts the engine. The rear compartment is full of paint cans, tarps and a ladder.

He has to steady himself, get his breathing under control, before he can drive. His shoulder is burning.

He leaves the van in an empty shopping plaza two miles away, calls Cosmo from the cell phone.

———

Cosmo watches from the doorway as Travis pulls off his gloves, runs water in the bathroom sink. He shrugs out of his jacket, dips his head under the flow. Crusted blood washes away, swirls pink down the drain. The pain sharpens.

She could have crushed your skull out there, he thinks. Another swing or two would have been all it took. But she didn't do it, and didn't call the police afterward. Did she think she'd killed him?

He pulls a bath towel off the rack to dry his head. It comes away pink with blood.

"You're in bad shape," Cosmo says. "This is no good, staying here."

"We're okay. No one knows where I am." He snapped the driver's phone into pieces on the way here, dropped them out the window. "How much fent is left?"

"Six caps. That's the last of it."

"Already cut?"

"Yeah, with powdered baby aspirin. It's cut heavy. I tried to stretch it out as much as I could."

"Get me one."

"You sure about that?"

Travis looks at him.

"All right," Cosmo says, and leaves the doorway.

Travis pulls off his T-shirt and peels the dressing away from his shoulder. It's bright with blood.

He hears Cosmo opening the floor safe in his bedroom. When he comes back in with a capsule, Travis twists it open, carefully taps a few grains onto the back of his left hand. He snorts them, feels the burn in his sinuses. He licks up what's left on his skin, then closes the capsule. He'll keep it for later.

Looking in the mirror, he's angry at himself. The money was there, she was there. It should have gone the way he planned. Instead it all fell apart.

No use going back to the condo in Howell. They won't be there anymore, and if they've gone to the police, someone might be watching the house. Cops may have already found the Saturn. He'll need to steal another car, one that won't be reported anytime soon. Then he needs to find a gun.

"You look like you're ready to drop," Cosmo says.

The fent starts to kick in. Now he wants rest, sleep.

"Not yet," he says.

THIRTY-SIX

KEITH DRIVES HER back to where she left the rental car. He's quiet the whole way. They stopped at the inlet, and she took their cell phones and the .25, dropped them over the seawall into the water. All that connects them to what's happened.

She slept four hours, woke feeling tired and weak. Her face isn't swollen anymore, but the bruise there is purple and yellow. There are finger marks on her throat.

He pulls up a block short of the car. The beachfront streets are still empty. No cops waiting, watching.

His hands twist on the wheel.

"What?" she says.

"Last night. I'm sorry. There was nothing I could do. If I could've gotten the drop on him, I would have. I never had the chance."

"Don't blame yourself for what happened," she says. "Blame me."

"What about the gun?"

"What about it?"

"You use it?"

"Do you really want to know?"

"No, I guess not."

"Then don't worry about it."

She takes the sports bag, gets out, watches him drive away.

She locks the bag in the trunk of the rental, looks toward the ocean. The water is calm. No wind now. Gulls swoop in the bright and cloudless sky. The night before seems like a dream.

She doesn't want to look. Doesn't want to go out there again but knows she has to.

And if he's still there in the sand, dying or dead, what will you do then?

She walks back toward the beach house, moves through the dune grass. The beach is empty. There's no sign of their struggle. The wind's swept away their footprints.

He's alive.

———————

"We should call the police," Annalisa says.

They're in the social worker's office. Joette bought a new cell phone, called the nursing home. If Travis Clay is looking for her, it's the only connection he has to her now.

"Not yet," Joette says. "I might be overreacting. But I wanted to be careful, make sure." She's given Annalisa his name and description.

"Who is this man exactly?"

"Someone I was involved with in a business deal. It went bad."

"And for that you think he might mean your mother harm? Why?"

"I don't know that he would," Joette says. "But I don't want to take the chance. I just wanted someone here to know, keep an eye out."

"No one gets in here without signing in, showing ID, saying what they're here for or who they're visiting," Annalisa says. "Security will detain anybody inside the building without authorization. We take the safety of our residents very seriously. If this Clay comes here and tries to get past the desk, we're calling the police, regardless. I'll make sure everyone on staff has his description."

"Thank you. It might be there's no reason to worry after all."

"We won't take that chance," Annalisa says. "If that man shows up here, he's leaving in handcuffs."

———

Her mother looks up at her, but there's nothing behind her eyes. She's propped up on pillows in the Geri chair in her room, wrapped in a blanket.

A knock at the open door. It's Lourdes from nursing.

"Kim told me you were here," she says. "We were starting to worry. Can I come in?"

"I'm sorry. I've been away."

"Are you all right?" She's looking at the bruise. Joette's sweater hides the finger marks on her neck.

"Walked into a door," she says. "Has she been eating?"

"Only a little bit today, but she's managed to keep it down, which is good. We had her on an IV earlier this week, to get her numbers up. But as soon as we take her off, they go down again. I think we may be approaching the point we spoke about."

"Hospice."

"There isn't much we can do for her now, except try to make her journey as peaceful as possible."

She might have died, and you wouldn't have been here, wouldn't have known.

"Talk to her," Lourdes says. "That can be comforting for her, even if she can't respond."

When Lourdes leaves, Joette leans over and kisses her mother's cheek. "It's Jo, Mom. I'm right here."

Her mother blinks; her dark eyes are glassy.

"I'm not going anywhere," Joette says. "And I'll never leave you alone again."

Driving back to the hotel, she's exhausted, with a fatigue deep in the bone.

She puts the money back in the safe, looks at it before she closes the door. Drug money, more than likely, she knows. But if she'd gone to Noah early on, told him everything, the police would have seized the cash. It would be sitting in a basement evidence locker somewhere, or already absorbed into some department's budget.

You almost died for this money. Maybe the only person it belongs to now is you.

She'll make the round of banks again, distributing the money back into safe boxes and accounts. Taking her time, spreading it out.

Phone calls to make. Glad now she kept up the insurance on the trailer. The company will likely write it off as a total loss, cut her a check. She'll junk the Subaru. The cost of four new tires would be more than the car is worth. She'll buy a used one that won't attract attention, pay cash. Then she'll need to find a place to live.

Welcome to your new life.

The next afternoon, she meets Helen at the diner. It's 3 p.m., and the lunch crowd has thinned out. Most of the booths are empty.

"How much of this are you going to tell me?" Helen says.

Joette stirs sugar into her coffee.

"I'm sorry I had to run out on you. I didn't want to leave you with that responsibility, but there was no one else I could trust."

She looks out the window into the lot, half expecting to see him out there.

Is this what it's going to be like? Looking over your shoulder until the day he finds you?

"Your face," Helen says.

"Took a fall."

Helen frowns. "I was waiting to get a phone call, with some news I didn't want to hear."

"It wasn't fair, leaving you in the dark like that. But it seemed like the best thing at the time."

"I'm scared to ask what happened."

"Maybe you shouldn't."

Helen crosses her arms, sits back. "Who are you, anyway?"

"Same person I always was."

"I don't think so."

The waitress refills their cups.

"Thanks for looking in on my mother," Joette says.

"How was she yesterday?"

"Weaker."

"Did she know you were there?"

"I don't think so. She was asleep most of the time. At this stage that's a blessing, I guess."

"Jo, anything you need from me, you only have to ask. You know that, right?"

"I do. Thank you."

"But promise me you'll never run off on me like that again."

"I promise," Joette says.

THIRTY-SEVEN

———

T RAVIS WALKS THE side of the highway, past the feeder ramps that lead to the Turnpike. Cars raise dust as they speed by. The setting sun flashes off planes circling the airport, lining up to begin their descent.

His head is a dull ache. He slept most of the previous day, then took another hit off the fent capsule that morning.

Horns sound as he sprints across the four lanes of the highway. He took the train from Middletown to Elizabeth, walked the half mile to the off-site parking area. It's a three-acre dirt lot fenced with chain-link and razor wire. Cheaper than the official airport lots, but farther away. The office is a small trailer. No shuttle van outside, so it's either on its way to the terminals, or coming back.

He walks through the open gate, down a rank of cars, stops at an old gray Impala near the back of the lot.

Leaning close on the driver's side, he takes off his belt, feeds the buckle through the gap between the window and door frame. He maneuvers the belt until the buckle catches the lock stem. It slips free on his first two tries. On the third, it holds fast, pops the lock. He opens the door and gets in.

The flathead screwdriver he brought with him is all he needs. He jams it into the ignition slot, smacks it deeper with the base of his hand, then twists the handle hard. The ignition lock cracks, and the car comes to life. The engine runs rough at first, threatens to stall. He gives it gas until the idle smooths, then drives toward the gate.

A security guard in a parka comes out of the trailer, holds up a hand for him to stop. Travis puts down his window.

"You're supposed to check in at the office," the guard says. "Get your keys."

Travis holds out a hundred-dollar bill. "Had an extra set."

The guard looks at the bill, then at the screwdriver in the ignition. Travis waits.

"Yeah, I guess you did," the guard says, and takes the bill.

Travis drives out.

———————

"Where's your truck?" Darnell Jackson says.

It's dark. They're in the Impala, parked in the McDonald's lot outside Camden, traffic rushing by. Darnell came alone in the Navigator.

"Traded up," Travis says.

"Looks like you got *fuck*ed up, too."

Travis looks in the rearview. He's taped a gauze patch over his temple, but the center of it has darkened, and the skin around it is bruised. His shoulder is stiff and warm, painful to the touch. He doused the wound with alcohol before dressing it again.

"You bring what I need?"

Darnell leans forward, reaches behind and takes a snub-nosed .38 from his belt, holds it out butt first. It has a scuffed blue finish, scratches on the barrel. The mother-of-pearl grips are wrapped with black electrical tape.

"This a joke?" Travis says.

"Best I could do."

"How many bodies this thing got on it?"

"Nothing recent, tell you that. You want it, it's yours."

Travis takes the gun. It feels out of balance. It'll be good enough at close range, undependable at anything more than a few feet. He opens the cylinder, shakes the six bullets out into his palm.

"Still waiting for you to come up with some more of that pure," Darnell says. "That ever gonna happen?"

"Soon."

"You need some extra cash, I might be able to help you out."

"How?" Travis reloads the gun, spins the cylinder to make sure it rotates freely, then snaps it shut.

"Put in some work."

"For you?"

"For my boy Joffo. Your kind of work, though."

"What's that mean?"

"It's a trap house. That old motel out there off 295 in Moorestown. Had a fire, been closed for years."

"I think I know it."

"They working out of one of those cabins in the back. Can't see it from the road."

"Competitor of yours? Can't handle it yourself?"

"Easier this way."

"Easier for you."

"My boy told me to put it out there, see what you say. Any cash you find there, you can keep."

"They black or white?"

"White boys. Peckerwoods up from Virginia, selling that oxy. Every few months they been coming up here, slinging their shit. They already been warned off."

"But they came back."

"Didn't get the message."

"Easier for me to get close to them, that what you're saying?"

"You tell them you're there to cop, you can walk right in."

"And I take the heat afterward," Travis says.

"These are tough times. All your recent troubles, thought you could use the work."

"Not that tough," Travis says. "Price is ten grand, cash, up front."

"I'll have to talk to my boy."

"Nothing to talk about. That's the price. In advance."

Darnell gives that a moment, nods. "I think he'll go ten."

Too quick, Travis thinks.

"Tomorrow," he says. "I'll call you when I'm ready to meet. You have the cash. Then I'll do this thing for you."

"I can tell my boy you're on it?"

"You can," Travis says.

———

He parks three blocks from Cosmo's place, kills the engine and leaves the screwdriver in the glove box. He cuts through alleys and yards, comes in through the kitchen.

Cosmo is sitting at the table there, talking low on a cell phone, his back to Travis. When he ends the call, Travis says, "You ought to keep that door locked."

Cosmo jumps, turns to him. "Jesus, T. You scared me."

Travis walks past him to the refrigerator, gets a Budweiser. He opens it, holds it out.

Cosmo shakes his head. "No, you're right. I need to watch the drinking."

Travis takes a seat. Cosmo's face is puffy, his hair lank and uncombed. His clothes are loose from weight loss.

"Who was that on the phone?"

"The shop."

Travis looks up at the clock. It's almost ten. "This late?"

"They wanted me to know they had a problem with one of the washers. A bad leak. Repair guy's coming tomorrow."

"Who runs the show when you're not there?"

"Esme, most times. I have someone else I bring in on weekends if I need him."

"This Esme, she know about us? The money you move through the business?"

"No, she doesn't know anything."

"She ever ask about me?"

"I told her you were an investor who liked to come by every once in a while, check on the shop."

Travis drinks beer. "Smart. I got some more cash coming in soon. We can add it to the fifty."

"From where?"

"Darnell Jackson."

"You and he got something going again?"

"Maybe. If it works out."

"You still trust him?"

"No reason not to."

"You need me to get involved?"

"You've got enough to worry about, don't you?"

"Can't help it."

"Relax," Travis says. "I have the feeling this is gonna work out for all of us."

THIRTY-EIGHT

THIS MY BOY Joffo," Darnell says.

Travis turns to the man in the Navigator's backseat. He's older than Darnell, wearing a black knit watch cap, a black-and-red leather coat.

They're under a Turnpike bridge in the Meadowlands, parked behind the Impala. He picked the place this time. There's black and silent swamp on both sides. Traffic rumbles by above, headlight reflections moving across the surface of the water.

"Darnell tell you the deal?" Joffo says.

"He did."

"So we good on this?"

"We are. Got my cash?"

"Darnell."

Darnell hands over an envelope. Travis opens it, counts the bills. Ten grand in hundreds.

"I need a day or so," he says. "Watch the way they're doing business, figure out the best approach."

"Nah, man," Joffo says. "No good."

"Why not?"

"What we heard, they pulling out tomorrow," Darnell says. "Going back home."

"Isn't that what you want?"

"No, they been warned once," Joffo says. "They need to go. We let them leave, they'll be back again. Maybe with some more boys. Might not be as easy next time."

"What are you saying?"

"Gotta be tonight," Darnell says, and looks at him.

"No way. I need to plan."

"What's to plan?" Joffo says. "You get up in there, and you do it."

Travis looks back at him. "You're disrespecting me a little here."

"No disrespect," Darnell says. "Just the way it is."

"We can go another thousand," Joffo says. "Get it to you tomorrow. But those boys gotta go tonight."

"Another thousand?" Travis says. He sits back. "Well then, that's all right."

He puts away the envelope, takes out the .38, sticks the muzzle into Darnell's armpit and pulls the trigger.

The sound fills the Navigator. Joffo's hand goes under his jacket. Travis twists to aim the gun at him. "Uh-uh."

Joffo's hand comes out slowly. "Lookit, man, I don't know what you're thinking, but—"

"Don't embarrass yourself."

Joffo's left hand moves closer to the door latch.

"How far do you think you'll get?" Travis says. "Or maybe you think it's worth taking the chance anyway."

Joffo shakes his head, looks out the window, then back at him. "Fuck *you*, cracker. You're the one been messing with everyone's business, dropping bodies. You brought heat down on everybody."

"Who's at that trap house tonight? More of Chano's people?"

Joffo doesn't answer. Travis thumbs back the hammer.

"The Ds put the word out on you," Joffo says. "You fucked things up for everybody. Chano had a lot of friends. You'll never get them off your ass."

"They pay you to get me up there?"

Joffo sits up straighter, squares his shoulders. "If you gonna do it, bitch, then do it. Or are you just gonna—"

Travis fires. Blood spots the back window. Gunsmoke drifts against the headliner.

He reaches into Joffo's jacket, careful to avoid the blood, pulls out a sleek black Bersa .380. He sets it on the console, pats him down, finds a diamond-studded money clip in his front pants pocket. The bills are all hundreds and fifties. He takes the clip. He'll count them later.

Darnell has five hundred dollars in a billfold inside his jacket. Travis takes the money, wipes down what he's touched, gets out. His ears are still ringing from the shots. He pockets the Bersa, throws the .38 out into the water, hears it splash.

He gets into the Impala, cranks the ignition, swings the car around. He drives past the Navigator, onto the service road and back up to the highway.

———

The town house is dim when Travis gets back. Cosmo's bedroom door is closed.

Travis sits at the kitchen table in the silent house, takes out the Bersa. There are seven rounds in the clip, the chamber empty. The gun smells faintly of oil. He pulls back the slide. The action is smooth. He slips the magazine back into the grip, jacks a round into the chamber, lowers the hammer.

Joffo was right. He was burned here. Sooner or later, the Dominicans, the bikers or Joffo's own people will get lucky, find him. Or find Cosmo, try to get to him that way.

It's time to move on, get out of Jersey, go somewhere else, start again. But he'll need a stake, enough cash to keep him going until he finds another hookup. What's in the safe won't cut it. He needs the rest of his money.

———

A noise pulls him from sleep. Sounds behind the wall in Cosmo's bedroom. Someone moving around in there, trying to be quiet. He hears a click, knows the sound. The mechanism of the spring panel that hides the floor safe.

He slips out of bed, pulls on jeans and a T-shirt, takes the Bersa from the nightstand. The clock there says 2 a.m. He goes out into the dark hallway. There's light showing at the bottom of Cosmo's door.

More noise, the soft thunk of the safe being closed, the click of the panel being pushed back into place.

The light goes out. The knob turns slowly as the door eases open. Cosmo comes out, turns to pull the door closed behind him. He's carrying the knapsack.

"You should have done that while I was gone," Travis says.

Cosmo stops, his back still turned.

"I can't deal with this anymore, T. I'm sorry."

"I understand. But half of that's mine, isn't it?"

Without turning, Cosmo holds out the knapsack. "Take it. All of it."

Travis goes around him into the kitchen, turns on the overhead light.

"Put it down," he says. "We'll talk about the money later."

Cosmo sets the knapsack on the floor. Travis tucks the Bersa into the back of his belt under his shirt, nods at the kitchen table. Cosmo sits, his face pale, looks at the floor. "It's too much for me, T. I thought I could hack it, but I can't."

"You've been having a hard time, I know. It's not the way I wanted things to go either. But you need to tell me what you were planning to do after you left."

"Go somewhere for a while, that's all. Wait for things to calm down."

"Leave all this behind? The shop, the house?"

"If I had to."

Travis shakes his head. "You're too smart not to have something else lined up. Maybe you thought things would go bad for me. That you could wait it out, go back to your life after I was gone."

"It wasn't like that."

"Look at me. Don't be scared."

Cosmo looks up. His eyes are shiny.

"What about clothes?" Travis says. "You pack a suitcase at least?"

"It's at the shop."

"So you did have a plan. All I want to know—and I need you to be honest with me—is if that plan included a phone call to your buddy in the state police."

"No, of course not. I'd never do that. You know me. You've got nothing to worry about from me. Ever."

Travis pulls out a chair, sits. "I've been thinking about what you said, about cutting our losses. You're right. Took me a while to realize that. We've played this out. What you want, isn't it? Go chase the straight life? Real estate, whatever? Now's your chance."

"You mean that?"

"Why not? You've put up with a lot. Seen a lot."

"We both have."

"True enough."

"Our luck went bad, T. We just have to accept that."

"Were you going alone?"

A moment's hesitation. "Yes."

"What about the woman at the laundromat? Esme. You tell her what you were going to do?"

He shakes his head.

Travis is suddenly tired again. He gets up, crosses behind Cosmo, runs water in the kitchen sink. He drinks a palmful, splashes some on his face. His shoulder burns.

"What about you?" Cosmo says. "Where will you go?"

"Not sure yet. Some things I need to take care of here first."

"The woman? It's not worth it. Forget about it. Walk away."

"I don't think I can do that."

"That money was lost the day Tommy took it. Everything that's happened since...where's it gotten us?"

"Too late now," Travis says. He shuts off the water. "You got a maid comes in?"

"Once a week. I called her yesterday, said I was going away, didn't need her for a while. I didn't want her to come here, see you."

"Good thinking."

He dries his hands on his jeans, then reaches under his T-shirt and slips out the Bersa. He points it at the back of Cosmo's head. "Don't turn around."

Cosmo stiffens, puts his hands on the table. "You don't have to do this."

"Yeah, I do."

"I've never gone against you, T. I never would. I swear on my mother."

"Might be a different situation now, all that's happened."

"It's not."

Make it quick, Travis thinks, between heartbeats. *You owe him that much.*

"Don't do this," Cosmo says.

"There's nothing to be scared of. Just close your eyes."

"This isn't fair," Cosmo says. Tears in his voice.

"I know," Travis says, and squeezes the trigger.

———

It takes all his strength to drag Cosmo into the bathroom, get him up and into the tub. Then he has to sit on the edge until he catches his breath. He draws the shower curtain, closes the door behind him.

At the front window, he looks out on the street. The town houses are far enough apart that a neighbor might not have heard the single shot. He waits, listening for sirens. The night's quiet.

He checks Cosmo's cell phone. It's locked, password protected. No way to know who he was calling.

The knapsack goes back in the safe. It'll be there when he needs it.

He's exhausted now. He shuts off the kitchen light, goes into the bedroom. He leaves the door open so he can hear, sets the Bersa on the nightstand and stretches out on the bed. He holds his hands up above him in the darkness until they're still once more.

———————

Waking, it all comes back to him. Where he was. What he's done.

The gray light of day fills the windows. In the hallway, there's blood on the carpet he didn't see the night before. Drag marks. Drying blood on the kitchen floor and table. A coppery smell in the air.

He changes his dressing in the bathroom, looks in the mirror at the closed shower curtain behind him. Something else the woman has to pay for, what she made him do, the corner she forced him into. All this is on her.

He knows then what he'll do that day. How to find her, flush her out, get the money. The only way left.

THIRTY-NINE

I T'S AFTERNOON WHEN Joette gets to the nursing home. She returned the rental, took a cab to a Toyota dealership on Route 36 in Eatontown. She picked out a five-year-old Corolla, had them draw up the paperwork while a salesman drove her to the bank. She got a cashier's check for $17,000, signed it over to the dealership, drove the car off the lot.

In her mother's room, one of the hospice aides, a young Black woman, is sitting beside the bed, reading a nursing textbook.

"Has she been sleeping all day?" Joette says.

The aide dog-ears her page, closes the book. "She ate a little lunch, but not much. I'm not sure about breakfast, you'll have to check with the nurse. I know Alora had her up in the activity room this morning. They had a singer there today."

"I'll stay with her awhile, if you want to go."

"Thanks." She gathers her things. "I still have a lot of studying to do. Taking my CNA certification test next week."

"You want to be a nurse?"

"An RN, eventually. If I can get enough financial aid."

"Good luck with that."

When she's gone, Joette takes her chair. Her mother is breathing softly, peacefully. Joette watches her sleep.

———

Joette wakes from a bad dream she can't remember. There's a light tapping on the open door. Clea, the front-desk receptionist, is standing there.

"Hi, Jo. I didn't mean to wake you."

"Sorry. I must have just drifted off." She straightens in the seat. Her back is stiff from the chair.

Clea holds out a white business envelope. "Someone dropped this off at the desk for you earlier. I meant to give it to you when you signed in."

"For me?"

She gets up, takes the envelope. It's sealed. Her name is written on the front in blue ink. There's no address.

"When did this come in?"

"Just a couple hours ago. A man dropped it off."

"A man?" A cold current of dread runs through her. "What did he look like?"

"I only saw him for a minute, and I didn't get a good look at him. The lobby was a little crazy. The EMTs had to take Mr. Lefferts to the ER at AtlantiCare, and there was a problem with his oxygen. They had to get him stabilized right there in the lobby before they could put him in the ambulance."

"This man say anything?"

"No. He was in and out. And I didn't actually see him drop it off. After things calmed down and the ambulance left, I found it on the desk. I know it wasn't there before, so it must have been him. I guess he just left it and walked out. He didn't try to come past the desk, or I would have stopped him. Is there a problem?"

"No," Joette says. "It's fine."

When Clea leaves, Joette sits back down. There's an odd weight to the envelope. She works a thumb into the flap, carefully peels it back and away.

Inside is a single sheet of paper, folded into thirds. She takes it out, sees the phone number written on it. When she unfolds the sheet all the way, something shiny slides out, falls into her lap. A razor blade.

FORTY

HE WAS HERE.

She goes out to the car, keys the numbers into her phone. When the line opens, she says, "I got your message. Don't go near her. I have what you want."

"All of it?"

"Yes."

"Surprised to hear from me?"

"No."

"You knew it would come to this, didn't you?" he says. "Back there on the beach, you should have hit me a couple more times, finished the job. But you didn't have the stomach to see it through. Second time you made that mistake."

He's driving. She can hear engine noise.

"I know where your mother is. She's not going anywhere soon. You might move her, but it'll take a while, and I'll find her eventually. I've got nothing but time. And I know where your friend dances. Even if she doesn't go back there, she'll turn up someplace like it. I'll track her down. The boyfriend, too, and the kid. All of them. You believe me?"

"Yes."

"Keep that in mind, it'll simplify things. You take off, I say, 'Okay, fine, sure,' and I kill somebody. Your fault. You hold back some of the cash, or maybe decide to go to the cops after all? I kill someone else. Your fault again."

"So I give you the money, and you kill me instead."

"You've cost me too much. No way you walk out of this, however it plays. But I promise you this. You fuck with me again, and even after you're dead, I'll keep going, just on general principles. I'll kill them all, not think twice about it."

"I'll do it. I'm tired of running."

"It was your call," he says. "You rolled the dice."

"It'll take me time to put it all together. Most of it's back in banks."

"I think you're lying about that. I'd bet you're still carrying it around, keeping it close. Either way, you better get it fast. I'm going to call you tomorrow night, tell you where and when. You don't answer, we're done. You don't do exactly what I say, we're done. Anything happens I don't like, we're done. Then I start keeping my promise."

"I'll answer. And I'll do whatever you want."

"I know you will," he says, and the line goes dead.

He ends the call, turns onto Cosmo's street. Two blocks away, a cluster of police cruisers are parked outside the town house, along with a crime scene van.

He slows, pulls over. Two cops are standing in the driveway, next to a pale blue Mercedes. Neither of them looks his way. It takes him a moment to remember where he saw the car before. Parked outside the laundromat. Esme's car.

He backs the Impala up slowly, reverses into a driveway. One of the cops lights a cigarette. They still haven't noticed him.

You almost drove right into it, he thinks. *It would have been all over. You fucked up, made a mistake coming back here. Lose your edge and you lose your luck.*

He imagines how it might have gone. Cosmo planning to meet Esme after he took the money from the safe. She'd have come here today when she didn't hear from him, couldn't reach him, found his Lexus still in the garage. Did she call the police then, or did she have her own key? Did she go inside, find what Travis had left? If she'd come while he was still there, he would have had to kill her as well.

It doesn't matter now. They have the body, his prints all over the place, his Silverado in the garage. The only money he has now is what he took off Darnell and Joffo. Everything is fucked, and it's his own fault.

He takes out the Bersa. If the cops see him, come after him, he'll use it, hold court in the street. He won't run.

He turns left out of the driveway, heads back the way he came, driving slow, the gun in his lap. He watches the cops in his rearview until he rounds a corner and they're out of sight.

———

The residential hotel is two blocks from the Elizabeth train station, on a narrow street that dead-ends at a tractor-trailer lot, just under a Turnpike overpass. He's been here before, knows they'll take cash and not ask questions or want ID. The lobby is a threadbare carpet and a wooden counter, a dusty plastic tree and a rack of mail slots.

The stooped gray-haired desk clerk takes one of his hundreds without a word, hands him a key attached to a green plastic diamond.

Travis doesn't trust the narrow elevator, climbs the stairs to the third floor. The hall is filled with the acrid smell of someone cooking in their room. Muffled voices and TV noise come from behind the doors he passes.

His room has a single window that looks out on a barren side lot. In the tiny bathroom, he strips off his shirt. He stopped at a *pharmacía* a block away, bought first-aid supplies.

The dressing sticks to his shoulder when he tries to peel it off. He drips alcohol on it, the sting quickly turning to pain. The sodden gauze comes off slowly. His entire shoulder is red, the gauze black and yellow. A sickly-sweet smell comes from the wound.

He fishes out the fent cap from his pocket, shakes some more out onto his wrist and snorts it. Only a dusting left in it now. He wishes he'd taken the rest of the capsules from the safe. Another fuckup.

He dresses the wound again, then changes the bandage on his head. From the room next door, he can hear grunting, a bed squeaking.

He takes out the Bersa, ejects the magazine. Six rounds left. It'll be enough. Tomorrow night ends it. After he's settled with the Harper woman he'll be in the wind.

He aims at the mirror above the dresser and dry-fires twice at his own reflection.

FORTY-ONE

ARLY AFTERNOON. OUTSIDE the window of Joette's hotel room, the sky is heavy with the threat of snow. She sits at the desk and writes a letter on hotel stationery.

Helen:

If you're reading this, chances are that I'm dead. I'm leaving this with you so you'll know what happened.

I did something I shouldn't have, took some money that didn't belong to me. It was in the car that crashed outside the motel that day, the one that caught on fire. I found the money in the trunk. I took it and hid it. I didn't tell the state troopers. I'm not sure why I did it, but once I did there was no going back.

There's a man named Travis Clay who says the money belongs to him. He's the one that hurt Noah. He also threatened my mother, and Brianna and Cara at the motel. He won't stop until he gets that money.

I've put everyone around me in danger, and I'm sorry for that. I'm also sorry I couldn't tell you more about what happened. But now when you look back on it all, I hope you'll understand why. And that you'll forgive me.

I'm going to give him the money, there's no other way. Once he gets it, he'll kill me. I guess I've always known that.

I don't know how things got to this point. I could have given it to him early on, ended all this. I don't know why I didn't. If I'd known how it would end up, I never would have taken it in the first place. And no one would have gotten hurt.

I've let so many people down, lied to so many people, you included. You are the best friend I've ever had. I wish I had been a better one to you.

Please show Noah this letter. I've kept so much from him, and it's because of me that he got hurt.

I'm hoping once I give this man his money, he won't be a threat to anyone around me anymore. That he'll go somewhere and never come back. I don't want anyone else to pay for what I did.

Please look after my mother when you can. She doesn't have much time left, and I want her last days to be peaceful. Her DNR and other paperwork are all on file there at the nursing home. I've listed you as a family member, in case any last-minute decisions need to be made. I'm sorry to leave you with this responsibility, but you're the only one I can trust.

I'm sorry I brought this down on everyone. I'm hoping what I do now will end it. I can't tell you why I did what I did. I'm not sure myself. If I could go back and change things, I would. But I can't. And this is the only way out.

Love, Jo

She seals the letter in a hotel envelope, writes Helen's name and cell number on the front. She'll leave it on the desk here, propped against the lamp in plain sight. If she doesn't come back, someone will find it.

She takes the money from the safe, loads the sports bag one last time.

You should have let it burn.

He'll wait until night to call. He'll want her somewhere close but isolated. Somewhere he can leave her body.

It was always coming to this. You knew that. Time to pay for what you've done.

FORTY-TWO

———————

SNOW DRIFTS DOWN softly on the Impala, the flakes melting as they touch the still-warm hood. Travis is parked in the gas station lot, watching the motel on the other side of the highway. Baxter's station wagon glows red under the neon Castaways sign. The office is lit, but all the rooms Travis can see are dark.

It's eleven-thirty. He's been here a half hour. Long enough. He takes the Bersa from his jacket, flicks off the safety. It'll be louder than the Ruger would have been, but out here no one will hear the shots.

He gets out, tucks the gun in his belt, zips his jacket over it. He waits for a car to pass, then crosses the highway.

Flakes of snow swirl in the air. Once across the bridge, he moves into the trees, comes out below the sign. He's bathed in red.

Through the window, he sees Baxter asleep at the desk, head resting on crossed arms. There's a black-and-white movie on the TV.

Travis tries the door. It's locked. He taps gloved knuckles on the glass. Baxter doesn't stir. He taps again, harder. Baxter looks up then, sees him, sits up straight. Travis points at the door. A moment later, it buzzes.

Chimes sound as he goes in. He smiles. "Hey, man, how you doing? Slow night?"

Baxter squints, as if trying to place him. Travis unzips his jacket, draws the Bersa. "Step back from the desk."

Baxter looks at the gun, confused. Travis doesn't want to give him time to react. He moves past the TV, flips up the hinged section of the counter.

"What are you doing?" Baxter says. "You can't come back here."

He puts the gun in Baxter's side, grips the back collar of his shirt, pushes him through the curtained doorway into the back room. "On your stomach."

"There's no money here," Baxter says.

Travis kicks a leg out from under him, and he goes down hard. He touches the gun muzzle to the back of his head. "Lay flat. That's it. Arms back."

He sets the gun down, binds Baxter's wrists behind him with a zip tie. "Is there anyone else here? Anybody in the rooms?"

"No." He's out of breath.

"If there is…"

"There isn't."

Travis feels his pockets, pulls out a cell phone. He slams it hard on the floor twice, tosses the pieces away, picks up the gun again.

"Whether you're alive or dead when I leave is all the same

to me," he says. "You try to get up, start banging around in here, I'll hear you."

"I won't. Don't hurt me."

Travis opens the breaker box on the wall, starts tripping switches. The office lights go out.

———————

She jumps when she hears the phone. When she answers, Travis Clay says, "You ready to do this?"

"When?"

"Now."

"Where?"

"Where else?" he says.

FORTY-THREE

S**NOW FLASHES IN** her high beams, blows against the windshield, the wipers sweeping it away. She's wearing her down vest over a flannel shirt, has the heat turned up all the way, but is still trembling with cold. The bag with the money is on the passenger-side floor.

She slows as she nears the motel. The sign and all the windows are dark. Baxter's station wagon is alone in the lot.

End of the road.

Watching from the office, Travis sees the headlights, knows it's her. The car slows, as if she's making up her mind.

He checks the Bersa, pulls the slide back to see the round inside. He'll make her bring the money in first, see how much she's brought. Have her count it out for him, then put one in her head.

Wind blows snow against the window. He opens the door, wedges a metal trash can against it to keep it from closing and locking. Cold air fills the office. He steps out onto the pavement.

She turns slowly, pulls into the motel lot. Her headlights sweep across him. She's a dark silhouette through the windshield. He motions to her to stop, raises the gun.

———————

She sees him there, caught in her headlights, framed against the doorway. She brakes, her high beams reflecting in the office window.

He puts up his left hand. In his right is the gun.

No.

She takes her foot off the brake, stamps down hard on the gas.

———————

He hears the engine race as the car surges toward him. There isn't time to fire. Blinded by the headlights, he throws himself to the right, just as the front end smashes into the doorway. He lands hard on pavement, the gun flying from his hand. The door shatters, spraying glass inside. The car reverses sharply, brakes a few feet away, as if ready to come at him again. The last of the door glass collapses.

He rolls onto his stomach, looking for the gun, sees it against the door of room four. He tries to stand, and his left leg gives out. He falls, crawls across the pavement, gets his hand on the gun. Twisting on the ground, he aims with both hands, fires. The first shot takes out the driver's window. The second punches through the door below.

Pain in his leg, but it takes his weight. He limps toward the car, its high beams lighting up the office. He jerks open the driver's door, points the gun inside.

The car's empty. There's safety glass on the seats and floor. No blood. The wipers are still going, making a scraping sound against the glass. The passenger door hangs open.

—————

She runs into the office carrying the bag, hears gunshots behind her. She pushes through the curtain into the back room. Baxter is facedown on the floor, hands bound. She can't leave him.

She slings the sports bag up onto the supply shelf, takes down the box cutter.

"Joette, is that you?"

She kneels beside him. "Quiet. Hold still." She starts to saw at the plastic zip tie around his wrists, careful not to cut him.

"You need to get out of here," she says. "Run for the trees, fast as you can."

"What happened? Who is—"

The zip tie parts. She pulls him to his feet, shoves him hard toward the exit door. "Go!"

He pushes against the panic bar, almost falls as the door swings open. She watches him start toward the woods at a lopsided run.

She looks back at the curtain. He'll be coming through it any second. The bag is too heavy to run with. She'll never make the trees.

The master key card is on its hook near the breaker box. She grabs it on her way out the door.

———————

Travis leans into the car, shuts off the ignition and head-lights, pockets the keys, lets the door shut. All is dark and quiet again. Snow falls lightly around him.

She'll go through the building and out the back door, make a run for the woods. He goes into the dark office, glass crunching under his boots. The brochure rack is on its side, pamphlets strewn across the floor.

Behind the counter, wind billows the curtain. He pushes it aside, goes through. Baxter's gone. At the end of the corridor, the rear door is ajar.

Gun up, he steps outside into the wind. Baxter is almost at the trees, running awkwardly, his hands free. He's alone.

Travis takes aim, fires, but the shot goes high. Then Baxter's out of range, into the dark of the woods and gone.

There's a concrete patio back here, a propane grill with a vinyl cover, picnic tables and benches. Five rooms face this side, units six to ten. If the woman didn't run, she's hiding in one of them. There's nowhere for her to go now, no way to get past him.

He goes back into the hallway, gets the heavy aluminum flashlight he saw on a shelf. He thumbs the button. The beam leaps out.

———————

She waits in darkness, her back to the wall, trying to quiet her breathing, listening for him. She heard the single shot, hopes Baxter got clear.

What now?

She didn't know what she was going to do when she pulled into the lot. Something about the way he stood there, holding the gun, waiting. She thought of everything he'd done, all he might do, and her foot moved from the brake to the gas.

She saw him dive to the side, a second before the car hit the door frame. The impact threw her against the shoulder belt but didn't fire the airbag. She reversed to clear the doorway, unsnapped the belt, crawled across the seat and out the passenger door, pulling the bag after her.

She can hear him outside the room now, his labored breathing nearer.

Wind whistles under the door. She grips the box cutter and waits for him.

———————

Room six is closest. He listens at the door, then heel-kicks it just above the knob. The trim splits. On the second kick, the door flies open, smacks the wall behind it.

He shines the light inside, pans the beam across the room, tracking it with the gun, ready to fire. The closet door is open, the bathroom and kitchenette empty. No one in here.

Four rooms left.

———————

She hears the door to room six crash open, wood splintering. She holds her breath. The wind whines outside, changes pitch. She can feel her own heartbeat.

The next crash makes her jump. It's closer. Room seven. She's trapped. If she tries to run now, she'll be an easy target.

Another door gives way, closer still. Room eight. She hears him through the wall.

He stops outside room nine, listening again. He thought he heard a noise inside, breathing. Nothing now, except the wind.

You can walk away, he thinks. Get back in the Impala, head north. Find her some other day and do what he promised. It's dangerous to stay. Someone might have driven by, seen the car and the damaged door, called 911. Baxter might have gone for help. Police may already be on their way.

But she's here now, close. He can feel it. Two doors left. He won't let her get away again.

He takes a step back from the door, kicks it hard. Something cracks, but the frame holds. Another kick above the knob, putting his weight into it. Trim buckles. Wood breaks. With the third kick, the door swings open.

He points the gun into darkness, traces the flashlight beam across the walls, right to left and back again. The room is empty, but the bathroom door is closed. He trains the light on it, steps farther into the room.

Movement behind him. He swings around and there she is, coming out from behind the broken door, something in her hand. He gets the flashlight up to block it, feels the slash across his upper arm. The flashlight falls, rolls. He swings the gun toward her, fires too soon. A bright muzzle flash, and the bullet holes the wall. Then she's shoving him away, and he's falling, first against the bed and then onto the floor.

He raises the gun, but the doorway's empty. She's gone.

FORTY-FOUR

---

*R*UN.

A clear shot for him if she heads toward the trees. Instead, she races around the building, past the dark vending machines, back to the car. She pulls open the driver's door. The keys are gone.

Headlights coming down the highway. She drops the box cutter, runs out to the road, waves her arms. The car speeds up as it goes by, close enough that she feels its slipstream.

She hears him behind her, coming around the side of the office. She runs across the roadway, heading for the opposite shoulder, the ditch beyond, cover.

She's almost there when she feels the hard punch in her back. It drives the breath from her, sends her face-first down the slope, the ground rushing up. She tumbles into the ditch, the sound echoing behind her.

He shot you.

He sees her lurch forward with the impact, knows the shot was good. She falls out of sight.

He stands in the lot under the dark sign, panting in the cold air, snow blowing around him. He touches the rip in his jacket. He's bleeding. She cut him with something, but he deflected it with the flashlight. She was aiming for his throat.

In the distance, he can hear sirens. He crosses the highway. She's facedown in the ditch at the bottom of the slope, not moving.

"You fucking deserved that," he says.

The sirens are louder, rising and falling. They'll be here soon.

He goes back to her car, takes out the keys and unlocks the trunk, raises the lid. Inside is a spare tire, nothing else.

Way the dice fell, he thinks. *Nothing you can do about it.* She's dead or dying, and the money's gone for good, wherever it is. He tosses the keys away.

Flashing lights far off down the highway. If he runs for the Impala, he can make it, get away before a cruiser reaches the motel.

He starts down the road. Halfway across the bridge, he turns, looks back at the spot where she fell.

One bullet left.

Joette rolls onto her back, snow drifting down on her. Her left arm is numb, useless. A wet warmth spreads beneath her shirt. Blood.

She shifts onto hands and knees, hears sirens in the distance. She starts to crawl. If she can make it to the culvert she can hide there, wait for help to come.

"I should have known."

She looks up, and he's there on the shoulder just above, pointing the gun down at her.

The sirens are closer, louder. He steadies the gun with his other hand. She shuts her eyes.

Brakes screech. She hears car doors opening, voices shouting.

―――――

Travis looks down at her. Her eyes are closed. She's breathing hard, waiting for the bullet.

Blue-and-red rollers sweep across the wet ground. White spotlights catch him. A woman he can't see is shouting at him to drop the gun. Then comes the unmistakable sound of a pump shotgun being racked.

He squints into the glare of the lights, then looks back into the ditch.

"You got lucky again," he says. Then he turns toward the lights, raises the gun and fires.

―――――

Joette hears the pop of handguns, then the boom of something bigger. The pops keep coming, like a string of firecrackers, stopping as suddenly as they began.

She opens her eyes to a light shining down on her,

dim faces behind it. Then more lights, other faces, police uniforms. One of the cops is a woman. She has the butt of a shotgun braced against her hip. Joette recognizes her. It's Bryce, the state trooper from the day of the accident.

"Don't try to move," she says. "Ambulance is on its way."

Joette shudders. She's cold all over.

"Breathe," Bryce says. "Stay with us."

Joette looks up at the falling snow. Her eyelids flutter. She's growing sleepy.

Is this what it feels like to die?

The lights above her start to fade, the faces blur. She hears their voices from across a far distance, growing fainter, and she closes her eyes again.

FORTY-FIVE

WHEN SHE WAKES, she's in a hospital treatment room. Noah stands at the foot of the bed, the curtain drawn closed behind him.

She's been drifting in and out of sleep since they loaded her into the ambulance. She remembers an EMT cutting her vest and shirt away, the flannel sticky with her blood. Then being rushed down the hall on a gurney, looking up at the blur of ceiling tiles as they went past, wondering when she was going to die.

"You're back," Noah says.

Her mouth is dry, her lips chapped. Under the loose gown, her shoulder is thick with bandages. An IV bag hangs above her, the tube feeding into a needle in the back of her right hand. Monitors beep just out of sight.

She tries to sit up.

"Don't," he says.

She lies back. "Water."

"Nurse says just ice for now."

He takes a plastic cup from the bedside table, holds it to her lips. She sucks in crushed ice, lets it melt in her mouth. Up close, she can see the shadows under his eyes, all that's left of the bruising.

He takes away the cup. She shifts in the bed. Her shoulder is stiff, but there's no pain. Whatever they're giving her is working.

"Where am I?" she says.

"Jersey Shore in Neptune. They were the closest trauma center. How much do you remember?"

"Not much."

"The ER doctor stopped by a little while ago. You were sleeping again. He said he'd come back."

"How's Baxter?"

"Fine. Couple scratches, that's all. He says you saved his life."

She touches the dressing. "How bad is it?"

"Didn't they tell you?"

"They probably did. But I'm not sure how much I understood."

She gestures at the cup. He hands it to her, and she shakes more ice into her mouth, feels it cool her throat.

"Clean through and through," he says. "Round ricocheted off your shoulder blade, came out just above your collarbone. Soft tissue all the way. Missed your lung and a pretty major artery, they said. I'll let the doctor explain the rest."

She finishes the ice, sets the cup down, feels the first stab of returning pain.

"There are two troopers and a detective here," he says.

"They're going to need you to give a statement when you're ready. Is there anybody you want me to call?"

"No."

"Do you have a lawyer?"

"Do I need one?"

"Not a bad idea, have someone on your side from the beginning," he says. "Get your story straight."

"There's nothing to get straight. I got shot, by the man who was stalking me. The same one that hurt you."

"Why did you go to the motel?"

"He called me. He was going to kill Baxter if I didn't come there."

"How did he get your number?"

"I don't know," she lies.

"You should have called me, or 911."

"Maybe I should have. But I didn't."

She's tired again, wants to sleep. There are voices down the hall, growing nearer.

"Here they come," he says. "Last chance. Is there anything you want to tell me before they get here?"

He wants something, anything. To help explain things. To explain you.

"No," she says.

FORTY-SIX

DON'T THINK I know anyone else who's ever been shot," Helen says.

Late afternoon, and the diner's less than half full. Joette is finishing up a slice of apple pie, cutting at it with the edge of her fork. Her left arm is in a sling under her jacket. "I wouldn't recommend it."

"I'm surprised they let you go so soon."

They kept her two nights for observation, discharged her the afternoon before, with prescriptions for painkillers and antibiotics. She took a cab back to the hotel, tore up the letter, slept the rest of the day and night through. That morning, she rented another car. The Toyota had been impounded as evidence.

"It might be stiff after it heals, but I can deal with that," she says. "I have to follow up with a doctor, get the dressing changed, check for infection. That's it for now. Maybe some PT down the road."

"Do you have one?"

"What?"

"A doctor."

"Not yet. I'll find one."

"Two nights in the hospital, ambulance, ER. How much will all that cost?"

"I'll work it out somehow," Joette says. "Pay them as I can."

"How are you managing with all this? I don't mean physically."

"Haven't been thinking about it too much. The pills help me sleep. If I have dreams, I don't remember them."

"Something to be thankful for."

Joette sets down her fork. "You're giving me that look again."

"Am I? I'm just wondering if I'll ever know what all this was about."

"You know most of it."

"I doubt that. And I'm still trying to figure something else out."

"What's that?"

"Who you are now."

"You asked me that before. I haven't changed."

"Then there's a side of you I've never seen, many years as I've known you."

"Could be."

"That's your answer?"

"It's the only one I've got," Joette says.

———

Ten p.m. Steering one-handed, she pulls into the motel lot, parks under the dark sign. Plywood is nailed across the office door and crime scene tape is strung in front of the rooms, doorknob to doorknob.

She shuts off the headlights, waits as a car passes, then gets out, walks around to the back patio. More plywood across the broken doors there, more crime scene tape.

There's just enough moonlight to see by. She takes the vinyl cover off the propane grill, lifts the cast-iron lid. The sports bag is still there. She unzips it, looks at the money, remembers what Danny Boy said: *"You earned it."*

Did I?

She feels nothing, looking at the banded bills in the moonlight. Then she zips up the bag again, takes it out, closes the grill and replaces the cover.

The highway is empty in both directions. She stows the bag in the trunk, gets behind the wheel and drives away from there.

FORTY-SEVEN

HE NEXT MORNING, she parks outside Keith's apartment, taps her horn. Brianna comes out. Joette takes off her sunglasses, nods to the passenger seat.

A curtain moves in the apartment's front window, Keith looking out.

"How do you feel?" Brianna says when she gets in.

"I'm fine. I just wanted to talk to you alone. How's Cara?"

"Okay, I think. I hope. It's hard to tell. She was asking if you were all right. I didn't want to bring her to the hospital with me. I thought it might upset her, see you like that."

"That was the right call."

"I think sometimes kids get over things better than we do. It's easier for them to forget."

"Forgetting is good," Joette says. She takes an envelope from her sling.

"What's that?" Brianna says.

"A check for twenty thousand. For all you've been through."

"I can't take that. I owe you already."

"This isn't a loan. I did some things, made some choices, that put you and Cara at risk. Keith, too. I'm sorry about that. It was wrong."

"It wasn't your fault."

"Yes," Joette says. "It was. Take the money. Use it to find a place to live. Buy whatever Cara needs. Open a bank account, if you don't already have one. A friend of mine can help you with that."

"I don't know what to say."

"Don't say anything. Just take it."

Brianna puts the envelope in a jacket pocket. "Thank you. This will help a lot."

"You get into a jam later on, need more, let me know."

Brianna looks at the apartment, then back at Joette. "Are we okay now? Are we safe?"

"Yes," Joette says.

———

Her mother's eyes are closed. There's an oxygen mask over her nose and mouth. Joette can't tell if she's breathing.

"How long has she been like this?"

"She's been unresponsive since last night," Annalisa says. "When she wasn't any better this morning, we thought we'd better notify you."

She got the call after leaving Brianna, drove straight to the nursing home. Annalisa and Lourdes met her in the lobby.

"Her vitals weren't good, and she was having some respiratory discomfort as well," Lourdes says. "The oxygen's helping. She's breathing easier now. And she's in no pain."

Joette lays the back of her hand on her mother's forehead. Her skin is cool.

"We heard what happened to you," Annalisa says. "It was on the news. Thank God you're okay. The Lord must have been looking out for you."

"Maybe He was."

"The aides are here, if you'd like them to come in."

"No," Joette says. "I just want to sit with her for a while."

Annalisa leaves. Joette takes her mother's hand. A cloud shifts outside. Sunlight fills the room.

"I think she was waiting for you to get here," Lourdes says. "I see it all the time. They don't want to let go until they know their loved ones are safe and close. Tell her you're okay. That she doesn't need to worry about you anymore. That she can go in peace."

Joette feels warm tears on her face.

"There's nothing you can do now, except be with her," Lourdes says. "She's in God's hands."

"I don't want her to go. I'm not ready."

"She is," Lourdes says. "You've done everything you could for her. Now you can both rest."

───────

Joette's cell phone wakes her, buzzing on the hotel nightstand. She stayed at the nursing home until midnight, sleeping on and off in the chair beside her mother's bed, lulled by the low hum of the oxygen machine.

The phone screen lights up, shows her the time— 3:10 a.m.—and the number of the incoming call. It's the nursing home.

FORTY-EIGHT

O N A COLD and sunny morning three weeks later, Joette sits on the fender of her rental car, watching a yellow excavator maneuver in the motel lot. She's parked on the shoulder, just above the ditch where she almost died.

She can feel the vibration as the excavator backs up, treads clanking, and positions itself. Its long hinged arm swings right to left, and the heavy grapple at the end of it crashes into the side of the building. The front window shatters and collapses.

For a moment, she can see inside the office, the counter, the desk where she sat. Then the grapple's jaws close on a section of roof, tear it away with a screeching noise, and the ceiling caves in. The arm swings out over a blue construction dumpster and the grapple opens, spilling debris. Dust rises up.

A police cruiser comes down the highway, slows and pulls in behind her car. It's Noah. He gets out of the cruiser, closes the door, walks toward her. "Thought you might be here."

"Singh told me," she says. "I guess it was only a matter of time."

They watch the grapple slam into the building again. Part of the roof buckles and slides off in one piece, cascading into the parking lot.

He leans against her car door. "If that place could talk."

Dust floats across the highway toward them, dissipates in the air.

"I'm a little sad to see it go," he says.

"I'm not."

"How's the shoulder? I see you lost the sling."

"Aches a little, that's all. Thank you for coming to the funeral."

"I drove by your mom's house the other day. The For Sale sign was gone."

"I took it off the market. I'm staying there until I decide what to do next. I'll figure it out when I get back."

"You're leaving town?"

"Maybe, for a while. For now, at least. I just need to get away, get my head clear."

She turns to him, waits for him to meet her eyes. "Are we good?" she says.

"What do you mean?"

"I know the pressure all this put on you. I'm sorry for that. And I know you didn't get all the answers you wanted."

"Maybe some of them I don't want after all."

"Can you live with that?"

"I guess I'll find out," he says.

The grapple swings again. The last wall falls slowly in a wave of dust.

"There it goes," he says. The neon sign is all that's standing now.

She slides down off the fender. She's seen enough.

"You're a good man, Noah. Try to be happy."

"Easier said."

"But maybe not as hard as we think," she says.

———————

That night she drives down to the ocean, walks out on the fishing pier. The full moon lights a path on the water, stretching into the darkness.

She looks out at the waves, silver in the moonlight. She thinks of Troy and her mother, and Travis Clay, too.

They're all out there waiting on the other side. My ghosts.

Tomorrow she'll decide what to do, where to go. Now she's just tired.

Enough of the night, she thinks. *Go home.*

The moon behind her, she turns and walks back to her car.

ACKNOWLEDGMENTS

Many thanks to my editor, Josh Kendall, and to Sareena Kamath and everyone else at Mulholland Books/Little, Brown for their hard work and assistance, and to my agent, Robin Rue, for her unflagging support. Thanks also to the many friends, new and old, who brought some light to dark times. Love and respect to all.

ABOUT THE AUTHOR

Wallace Stroby is an award-winning journalist and the author of eight previous novels, four of which feature Crissa Stone, the professional thief labeled "crime fiction's best bad girl ever." His first novel, *The Barbed-Wire Kiss*, was a Barry Award finalist for best debut novel. A native of Long Branch, New Jersey, he's a lifelong resident of the Jersey Shore.